Her Amish Identity

(Originally published as
Love Impossible – Amish Dreams)

Jennifer Spredemann

To My Lord and Saviour, Jesus Christ.

To My Love and Saviour Jesus Christ

Unofficial Glossary
of Pennsylvania Dutch Words

Ach – Oh

Ausbund – German hymn book

Boppli/Bopplin – Baby/Babies

Dat/Daed – Dad

Denki/Danke – Thanks

Der Herr – The Lord

Dochder(n) – Daughter(s)

Englischer – A non-Amish person

Fraa – Woman, Wife

Gott – God

Gut – Good

Jah – Yes

Kinner – Children

Maed/Maedel – Girls/Girl

Mamm – Mom

Nee – No

Schatzi – Honey, Sweetheart

Vatter – Father

BOOKS by JENNIFER SPREDEMANN

AMISH BY ACCIDENT TRILOGY
Englisch on Purpose
Amish by Accident
Christmas in Paradise

AMISH SECRETS SERIES
An Unforgivable Secret - 1
A Secret Encounter - 2
A Secret of the Heart - 3
An Undeniable Secret - 4
A Secret Sacrifice - 5
A Secret of the Soul - 6
A Secret Christmas - 7 (aka 2.5)

AMISH BIBLE ROMANCES
An Amish Reward
An Amish Deception
An Amish Honor
An Amish Blessing
An Amish Betrayal

AMISH COUNTRY BRIDES

The Trespasser
The Heartbreaker
The Charmer
The Drifter
The Giver
The Teacher
The Widower
The Keeper
The Pretender
The Arrangement (releasing 2022 in the Amish Spring Romance collection)

UNLIKELY SERIES

Unlikely Santa
Unlikely Sweethearts
Unlikely Singing (More Amish Christmas Miracles collection)

OTHER

The Princess and the Prayer Kapp (Amish Fairy Tale 2-in-1 Collection)
Learning to Love – Saul's Story (Sequel to Chloe's Revelation – adult novella)
Her Amish Identity (formerly Love Impossible)
An Unexpected Christmas Gift (from the Amish Christmas Miracles Collection)
The Arrangement (Amish Spring Romance collection)

BOOKS by J.E.B. SPREDEMANN

AMISH GIRLS SERIES
Joanna's Struggle
Danika's Journey
Chloe's Revelation
Susanna's Surprise
Annie's Decision
Abigail's Triumph
Brooke's Quest
Leah's Legacy
A Christmas of Mercy – Amish Girls Holiday

Author's Note

It should be noted that the Amish/Mennonite people and their communities differ one from another. There are, in fact, no two Amish communities exactly alike. It is this premise on which this book is written. We have taken cautious steps to assure the authenticity of Amish practices and customs. Old Order Amish and New Order Amish may be portrayed in this work of fiction and may differ from some communities.

We, as *Englischers*, can learn a lot from the Plain People and their simple way of life. Their hard work, close-knit family life, and concern for others are to be applauded. As the Lord wills, may this special culture continue to be respected and remain so for many centuries to come, and may the light of God's salvation reach their hearts.

Author's Note

ONE

"Hey, what do you think you're doing? Get back here!" Sarah called out. She stood on the sidewalk, helplessly watching the entire frightening event unfold.

The enclosed gray buggy kept moving along the icy road, with not even a hint of slowing down. Had the driver even heard her?

She turned to the bystander beside her. "Did you see that? He nearly ran that little boy over!"

The older man nodded as though it were an everyday occurrence. How could he be so calm?

"Well, I'm going to go stop him!" Sarah began to race to her vehicle but paused momentarily. She turned and regarded the mother of the frightened young boy. "Will he be okay?"

"Yeah, he's fine. Just a little shaken up." The boy's mother stroked her son's fine chestnut hair.

Sarah moved out into the early morning traffic and passed a couple of vehicles. She couldn't lose that Amish buggy. She carefully swerved around one buggy, drove a couple of miles further, and then turned the corner to follow the madman.

"I can't believe he would do that! And then just go on his merry way," she fumed. "I thought the Amish were supposed to have more character than that."

The moment she caught up to the buggy, she noticed something peculiar. *What on earth?* There was no driver! At least, not that she could see. Sarah hastily rolled down her window.

"Hey!"

No response.

Oh, Lord. Is that thing empty? "Hey! Is someone in there?"

Sarah briefly deliberated. She couldn't just let the buggy continue on unmanned. What if someone got run over, like the little boy almost had? If she didn't stop this thing, *she'd* be the one responsible for any consequential tragedies.

"Whoa!" she called out to the horse from her window, attempting to keep her eyes on the road.

He kept on trotting. Didn't seem to pay any attention, in fact.

Whose buggy was it, anyway? Where was its

owner? Were they worried?

Okay, how did they do this sort of thing in those Wild West movies? She frowned. It couldn't be too difficult, could it? *What would Charles Ingalls have done?*

Without another thought, she accelerated slightly and quickly parked her vehicle on the shoulder ahead of the buggy. She'd thought about stopping directly in front of the buggy, but that could prove disastrous, especially if an oncoming car was in the other lane and the buggy attempted to pass. Who knew how the horse would react?

Sarah stood on the road's shoulder gathering her resolve. *Please help me, Lord.* She waited for the buggy to come near, then she attempted to grasp hold of the handle to catapult herself into the buggy's cab. Without enough thrust, her grip quickly loosened and she realized her dangerous position. She dangled by the buggy handle, her feet hitting the spokes of the wheel.

Oh, no! This is no time to panic, Sarah.

"Whoa!" she called out to the horse, emulating a male voice. *What have I gotten myself into?* "Please, God. Help!"

Miraculously, the horse slowed.

Sarah found the strength to pull herself up into the

buggy seat and, with shaky hands, yanked on the reins. Breathlessly, she whispered a prayer of thanksgiving. She attempted to steady her wildly beating heart. *Thank You, God.*

When the buggy finally came to a complete stop on the shoulder of the country lane, Sarah glanced into the back.

She gasped. A bruised and bloodied man, curled into the fetal position, lay on the buggy floor. She surveyed his clothing. He was Amish, alright. One of his suspenders had been nearly cut through. The hair under his black hat was trimmed in a bowl-shaped fashion as most Amish men she'd seen, and matched his walnut-colored beard.

What on earth happened to this man?

"Sir? Sir? You need to wake up."

He wasn't budging. Was he dead? She watched for a sign of life, then breathed a sigh of relief when his chest rose and fell.

She shook his shoulder gently at first, then with more force. "Mister. Wake up." The wind lifted the stench of alcohol and she quickly held her breath. Had this Amish man been drinking? Not that she knew anything about the Amish, but she was pretty certain they didn't approve of drinking alcohol.

The man groaned.

"Oh, good. You *are* alive." She momentarily debated what to do. Up ahead, she heard the clip-clop of an approaching buggy. Sarah hastily jumped from the buggy and pulled the horse to the fence. She loosely wrapped the reins around the top fence board. "Stay!" she commanded as though she were talking to a dog.

The oncoming buggy topped the hill, and Sarah waved her arms. The buggy came to a halt. *Thank You, Lord.* "Excuse me, there's an injured man in that buggy across the road. I think he needs help."

The buggy's male driver eyed her up and down and frowned in seeming disapproval. He stared at Sarah peculiarly for a good thirty seconds before speaking. "He needs *you.*"

"Oh no, I'm not a nurse or anything. I don't have any medical training." Or did he want her to drive him to the hospital?

"Jathan don't need no training, he needs his *fraa!*"

"His *fraa?*"

"Don't pretend you don't know, Sarah! You don't fool me with your *Englischer* clothes."

She frowned. This man knew her name? "Do I *know* you?"

He completely ignored her question. "What ya ought to be doin' is takin' him home. This is all *your* fault, you know! Jathan wouldn't be out if you'd come home sooner."

"I'm sorry, sir, but you must be mistaken."

"No mistake," he insisted.

"He really needs help. Please."

The man shook his head. "Your *kinner* are waitin'. Prob'ly been worried sick about ya. Go home, Sarah."

She sighed. This man was truly confused. Okay, she'd play his little game. "Where *is* home? I've...uh...forgotten."

The man's white beard bobbed on his chest. "Over the hill, chust two farms down, on the left. Big red barn."

She looked where the man pointed.

Without another word, he set his buggy in motion. No goodbye. No "Thanks for helping Jathan." Nothing.

Sarah looked over her shoulder as the man's buggy continued down the road. Her vehicle was too far away to go back now. *Oh, shoot! My purse is in the front seat.* Surely it would be fine out here in the middle of nowhere, practically. She hadn't seen one car pass by. This man really needed her help.

God, I'm going to play the Good Samaritan. Please keep an eye on my stuff.

She took the horse's reins and carefully maneuvered

the buggy back onto the seldom-traveled lane. As the horse trotted into the driveway, several Amish children spilled out of house. She counted—five girls.

Sarah looked at the oldest sympathetically. "Is this your father? He's hurt. He needs help."

They stared back at her and spoke to one another in Pennsylvania Dutch.

"You will not stay with us, *Momma*?" Tears surfaced in the teen girl's eyes.

"Honey, I'm not your mother."

The girl nodded adamantly. "*Jah*, you are. For sure and for certain."

Sarah disregarded the girl's notions and looked back at the injured man. There was something more important at stake here. "Will you help me get him into the house?"

The girl spoke again in their native tongue and the six of them carried their father into the house and set him on the couch. Sarah requested a cool rag for the man's face. "He needs coffee if you have some."

Sarah exhaled in relief when the man finally began to stir. "Will you sit here with him?"

The oldest girl nodded and Sarah moved to the kitchen to find a drink for herself and gather her thoughts. Asking for a ride back to her car was out of the question. She'd have to walk.

She reentered the living room, and found the man sitting up. "Sarah?" His eyes brightened and he seemed fully alert now.

Oh, no. Not him too. These poor people are sorely mistaken.

She ignored his word. "Oh, good. You're awake. I've got to be going now." Sarah moved toward the door.

He reached for her hand. "Please stay."

"I'm sorry, sir. I know I must look a lot like your wife, but I'm not her." She rushed out as quickly as she could.

As she walked back the direction she'd come, her heart began to pound. How far up the road did she leave her car, anyway? A sinking feeling struck when she topped the hill.

My car's gone! Who had taken it?

The buggy she'd seen earlier slowly approached from the opposite direction. The same elderly man stopped, beckoning her close. Did he know what happened to her car?

"I need to find a telephone," she said. "My car's gone."

He grasped her cold hands, which were now beginning to turn numb. "Come. It's time to go home now, Sarah."

8

TWO

Warmth covered Sarah's face but her eyelids remained shut. She really should be getting up. There was no telling how long she'd been asleep. *That was the strangest dream I've ever had,* she thought, in her semi-nocturnal haze.

The shuffling feet in another room told her that if she didn't arise soon, the children would leave for school without her bidding them farewell. Had Mark left for work already? Sarah abruptly forced herself to rise.

Oh, no! Her gaze traveled the room of the simple farmhouse. *This cannot be happening.*

"Sarah?"

She glanced up in the direction of the male voice and frowned. It was the man she'd rescued from the buggy. *Was that yesterday?*

"Oh, good. I thought you might sleep the whole

day away. The *maed* have already finished school for the day. They're choring now."

"I don't understand."

The suspender-clad man moved closer, and he sat on an ottoman near the sofa where Sarah sat. Apparently, he'd taken a bath since she'd last seen him, because he looked and smelled much better than the evening before. He took her hand and she stared at the rough callouses that marred his hands. Her first instinct was to pull away, but she sensed an urgency in his grip, so she refrained.

"I wish you wouldn't pretend you don't know us, Sarah."

"I *don't* know you."

"C'mon. These *kinner* are your own flesh and blood. Are you saying you don't know your own *bopplin*?"

She shook her head. "I'm not who you think I am. My name is Sarah Brewer. I live in Baltimore, Maryland. I have a family there—a husband and two children."

A forceful word escaped the man's breath, but she couldn't decipher its meaning. He reached for her ankle and began pushing up her pant leg.

Sarah quickly jerked her foot away. "What do you think you're doing?"

"*Nee!*" He reached for her leg again. "Let me show you."

Sarah frowned, but his calm demeanor placated her frazzled nerves. Somehow, she knew this man wished her no harm and could be trusted. "Okay," she hesitantly agreed.

His warm hands slid her denim pant leg up to her knee. "See, there."

She looked down and stared at the four-inch scar on the inside of her calf. "That was from a car accident."

He adamantly shook his head. "*Nee*, Sarah. You were helping me out in the field with the cattle. One of our heifers was having some trouble calving, so you ran back to the house to have the *kinner* call the neighbor over. When you jumped over the fence, you got this here cut on your leg."

"A lot of people have cuts on their legs." She swallowed. "I just happen—"

"Those aren't the only marks on your body, Sarah. How about...?" He leaned over and whispered in her ear.

Sarah gasped and protectively wrapped her arms around her chest. How could he possibly know about *that* birthmark? "I—"

"Sarah, you're my *fraa!* Please stop pretending you don't know it."

Sarah recognized the pain that tainted his eyes. *This poor man really does believe I'm his wife.*

But she couldn't let him continue this absurd notion. "Look, mister."

"Jathan."

"Jathan. I don't know what's going on, or how I got here, or why you think that I'm your wife. I really think you're mistaken. I'm not just *pretending* that I don't know you or your children—I *really* don't know you. Maybe I might look like your wife, but I'm not her." She arose from the couch. "And if you'll excuse me, I really do need to get back home. I'm sure my *husband* and girls are very worried about me."

"How long have you been married?"

The question caught her off guard. "To Mark? Oh, it's been about eight years now. Our girls are five and seven."

"You left us ten years ago. August second." Tears formed in Jathan's eyes. "I never thought we'd see you again. Thought I'd be a grass widower all my life. But I've been praying, and here you are. I miss you so much, Sarah. Please stay here with us."

Ten years ago? No, that can't be. Her heart raced. "I have to go."

"Sarah, I've changed! I'm not the man I used to be. When you left, God got a hold of my heart."

"I'm not your wife, but if I was, I certainly wouldn't believe *that* story. When I found you, you were out cold from alcohol consumption."

"*Nee*, I wasn't drinking." He thrust a hand through his already tousled hair. "I was out looking for you! Same as every night since you left. A couple of *Englischers* thought they'd use me as a punching sack. They didn't like Amish folks and they let me know it. *They* were the ones drinking."

"You reeked of beer."

He shrugged. "They must've poured it on me after they thrashed me. Sarah, the last time I drank was the night before you left. I promise you I've changed. You can talk to Bishop Wagler."

"I don't know what to say to you, Jathan. This whole situation is just preposterous."

"Say you'll stay." He dropped to his knees and his unsteady hand grasped hers. Did he have tears in his eyes? "Please, Sarah. I *need* you. I don't want to live the rest of my life alone."

The desperation in his voice nearly caused her to contemplate this outlandish idea. If she weren't married, she might actually consider the validity of his claims. "I'm not who you think I am. I told you I *have* a family."

"But *we're* your family, Sarah."

"I'm sorry. Really, I am. Goodbye, Jathan."

Sarah's hands still trembled as she now gripped her vehicle's steering wheel. She'd managed to find her car after speaking to the local sheriff's office. Fortunately, they'd agreed to release it free of charge, given her bizarre situation. They must've thought she'd lost her mind and took pity on her.

As she neared the exit toward Baltimore, Jathan's last words to her echoed in her mind. *I'll keep praying that God will bring you back to us.*

But that wasn't the only thing that plagued her conscience. He'd said she left ten years ago, which would have been right around the time of the accident. It couldn't be true, could it? Were they really her flesh and blood family? Just the idea that she could have another family seemed ridiculous, let alone an *Amish* family. And if it *was* true, then what? It wasn't like she would just abandon the only life she knew.

One thing was certain. She needed to get to the bottom of this mystery. If anyone knew the truth, her parents would.

THREE

Sarah pulled in a deep breath as Mark held her tight. His arms had engulfed her the moment she appeared on the doorstep.

"Honey, I'm so glad you're here. And that you're alive," he spoke the words into her hair and pressed his lips to the top of her head. "I've been worried sick. I was sure something dreadful had happened to you. When the police called and told me they'd found your car on the side of the road in the middle of nowhere, they assumed you'd been abducted. I can't tell you how frightened I've been. I don't think I've ever prayed more intensely."

"I'm relieved to be home too." But, was this *really* home? A million questions swirled in her mind. Would Mark have any answers?

"The girls don't even know you've been missing. Since it had been less than two days, I was holding out hope that the police would find you." He stared into her eyes. "Where on earth were you, Sarah?"

"It's a long story." Did she really want to tell him everything when *she* still had so many unanswered questions? "I was at an Amish home."

His forehead creased. "An Amish home? Seriously?" He chuckled slightly. "I've gotta hear this. How on earth?"

"Let's sit." They moved to the couch. "I know. It was very strange. I was in Lancaster, near the Thirty around Ronks. I'd just come out of the store and was heading to my car when this Amish buggy whipped around the corner and nearly trampled a little boy." She recalled the event in vivid detail. "I yelled after the buggy to stop, but it kept barreling down the road."

"That's crazy." Mark's expression widened.

"I know. Anyway, I was furious that the driver would just keep on going." She bit her lip. "You won't believe what I did."

"Oh, no. What?"

"What any other civilized human being would do. I jumped in my car and went after the buggy." She ignored her husband's amused expression. "When I caught up to it, I realized there was no driver."

"You're kidding."

"No. So, being the sane person that I am, I pulled a

Charles Ingalls and jumped into the buggy."

"No, you didn't." Mark laughed.

"I did. Seriously."

"I kind of wish I could've been there to see that." He chuckled.

"It wasn't funny. I was scared."

"I bet you were. So…"

"So, I was able to stop the buggy. It turned out there was a guy in the buggy, on the floorboard. He had been beaten up and was in need of medical attention. The horse knew the way home. I'm not sure what all happened after that except that I woke up on their couch this afternoon."

"Perhaps you overexerted yourself and collapsed."

"I must have."

"You know, that's the craziest story I've ever heard."

"Yeah, the sheriff thought so too." *If they only knew the half of it.* "Would you object to me visiting Mom today?"

"Can it wait till tomorrow? I want the girls to see you first."

"Of course. I'd planned on going after we have dinner, but I can wait till tomorrow."

"Come here." Mark reached out his arms and she stepped into them. "I don't ever want to let you go."

Sarah took a sip of the coffee her mother had offered her just moments before. She stared at her mother from across the kitchen table she'd sat at as a child. Or so she'd been told. "Mom, what was my life like before the accident?"

Her mother's eyes widened and her mouth slightly dropped. "Where did *that* question come from?"

Sarah shrugged. "I'm curious. We've never really talked about it before."

"Your father and I told you that it's probably best if you just move on. You don't need to know about the past. If you were supposed to remember, you would." Her mother sighed and patted her hand. "We've already told you the important things that you need to know."

Liar. Sarah wanted to yell the word. Heat rose in her cheeks.

She slapped her hands on the table. "Really, Mom? Really? You don't think that telling me that I had a *husband* and children was important enough to tell me?"

Her mother gasped. "Where did you hear about that?"

"So, it *is* true!" Sarah rose from the table, unable to stop the tears that pricked her eyes. "Why didn't you tell me?"

"How did you hear about this, Sarah?"

"From Jathan!"

Her mother's face turned a ghostly white. "Jathan—is *that* where you've been?"

Sarah nodded. "Mom, how could you and Dad lie to me? How could you allow me to marry another man?" She couldn't remember a time she'd been more upset with her parents.

"You don't understand, Sarah. There's a lot you don't know. Jathan's not a good man."

"It doesn't matter, Mom! I'm *married* to him. We have children together." Her breathing became shallow, like her chest might cave in.

"Sarah, if you'd just calm down—"

"I don't want to calm down! Mom, I can't be part of two families at the same time. Did you tell Mark any of this?"

"Of course, not."

With a shaky hand, she wiped a tear from her cheek. "What would Mark say if he knew I was married to another man? Mom, how could you and Dad think this was okay?"

"You left Jathan, Sarah. You didn't plan on going back." *Another lie.*

Sarah frowned. "I wouldn't have just left a husband and children."

"You did." Her mother sighed. "We warned you not to marry him in the first place, but you were stubborn. You wouldn't listen. Your father and I knew that the Amish and *Englisch* don't mix well. We'd heard of another family that had been through a similar situation and it hadn't worked out for them either."

Sarah wanted to storm out and never come back, but she needed answers. And, unfortunately, her mother and father were the only ones who held them. And perhaps Jathan. "Are Jathan and I divorced?"

"No. But the courts have no record of you being married to Jathan. I guess the Amish sometimes do things differently. This community kept their own private records back then."

"So, according to the Amish—and *God*—Jathan and I are still married."

"But not according to *our* laws." Had her mother always been this insensitive? Was that all she cared about?

"Our laws? What about my life?" her voice creaked. "What am I supposed to do now, Mom?"

"Just live the only life you know. That's all you can do."

"I don't see how I can do that now. The girls—mine and Jathan's children—they saw me. They know their mother's alive and well. And Jathan—Mom, he *still* loves me. He begged me to stay."

Did her mother just roll her eyes? "He's too late. He should have loved you years ago."

"He did. Mom, Jathan quit drinking the day I left."

"Is that what he told you?" she scoffed.

Sarah frowned.

"I think you should make an appointment with Pastor Joe. He'll be able to offer a bit of wisdom, I think."

"Does *he* already know about this too?"

"I've never mentioned it."

Sarah sighed. "I think I will."

Never would she trust her parents again.

FOUR

"I'm sorry, Sarah. But in this circumstance, I think divorce might be your only option."

Sarah eyed her pastor of five years from across his sleek cedar desk. "You're *counseling* me to get a divorce? Isn't that like sacrilegious or something?"

"In a normal circumstance, I wouldn't recommend divorce. But this isn't normal. This is actually one of the most—no, it is *the* most bizarre thing I've ever heard."

"Okay, so *who* do I divorce? Husband number one or husband number two?" She knew her question must've sounded flippant, but seriously?

"What does Mark think about all of this?"

"Mark has no clue that I'm married to another guy. He's probably going to flip out."

"But Jathan knows you're married to Mark?" Pastor Joe's fingers steepled in front of his chin.

"Correct."

"And how does he feel about it?"

"He wants me back. He said he's been searching for me every day since I've been gone."

"Every day? For ten years?" His mouth fell open.

Sarah nodded.

Pastor Joe leaned back in his chair. "Wow. I can safely say this is definitely the most unique situation I've ever encountered."

Sarah unclasped her hands. "I can't believe this is *my* life! How can I file for divorce when I've been taught that it's wrong for as long as I can remember? Doesn't the Bible say that God *hates* divorce? Isn't it like an abomination to Him or something? You're counseling me to do something that God hates!"

"I realize it's difficult. Divorce *seems* like the most logical solution. But the truth is, I don't know how to counsel you in this situation. At least, not with absolute certainty." His look of sympathy provided little comfort. "The best advice I can offer you is to pray about it, Sarah. Ultimately, *you're* the only one who can make this decision. And you'll have to live with the consequences."

"Mark, please sit down. I need to tell you something important." *If only Mom and Dad had thought this*

was important ten years ago!

Mark's brow lowered and he eyed his wife with concern. "What is it?"

"It's absurd, actually." Sarah laughed nervously and paced back and forth.

"You know I don't like charades. Just spit it out, Sarah."

"I'm married."

Mark smiled. "I know that, honey." He wiggled his fingers to remind her of the ring he wore.

"No. I mean, I'm married to someone else." There. She said it.

Mark frowned. "Are you feeling all right, honey?"

"Mark." She sighed. "I kid you not. I am married to another man. *And* to you too."

He shook his head. "That's not possible. Bigamy is against the law."

"I know."

"I'm not quite understanding this." He rubbed his forehead.

"Okay, remember I'd told you that I had a car accident before we met?"

He nodded slowly.

"Well, I had amnesia. I *still* have amnesia." She looked to see if he was following. "I didn't know that I had been married before the accident because I couldn't remember and no one had the decency to tell me."

Mark shook his head and Sarah understood his denial. She'd felt the same until harsh reality smacked her in the face.

"Well, where is he? Where's this other guy you're supposed to be married to?" He held out his hands, as though she could make Jathan appear out of thin air.

"He's Amish."

"Amish? Is that—"

"Yes, that's where I was. Jathan was the one I happened to rescue from the runaway buggy."

Mark raked a hand through his hair. "And you spent the night at his house?" His voice rose an octave.

"We didn't do anything." She assured him. "I thought he was crazy at first when he insisted I was his wife. And then when he said that I'd left ten years ago, well, I thought maybe there could have been some validation to what he was saying. So, yesterday, when I went to Mom's, she admitted that I was indeed married to Jathan before the accident. She and Dad thought it was best if I didn't go back to the Amish, so they tried to hide it from me. And they've succeeded up until now."

"You mean, you *were* married to him. You're not married to him *now*."

"No. I *am still* married to him."

"I don't believe this." Now Mark stood up and paced the room. "So, what? Do you have kids with this Amish guy too?"

Sarah nodded. "Five girls."

"Unbelievable!" Mark's voice rose.

"Don't be angry."

"I find out that my wife is married to another man and she says 'don't be angry.'" A sarcastic chuckle escaped his breath. "I think I have cause to be a little distressed."

Sarah remained quiet. It was probably best if she gave Mark time to absorb this new revelation.

"So, what now?"

"Pastor Joe advised me to get a divorce. He thought it would be the most logical option."

Mark released a pent-up breath. "That's probably best."

"But isn't it wrong? I mean, I love you and I'd *never* want to leave you and the girls. But I feel bad for Jathan and the other children—*my* children. How can I just abandon them? Especially now that they know I'm alive? Don't I have an obligation to them?"

"Well, wasn't he concerned at all about your whereabouts?"

"He said he's gone searching for me every night."

"You're kidding."

"No, I'm not. I guess he never knew about the accident. He just assumed I'd left—which, I *had* left."

"So, you left him?"

She shrugged. "Apparently. I don't know. I can't see myself just leaving the kids behind too, especially if Jathan was drinking."

"Were you saved?"

"I have no idea. I don't think the Amish believe you can be saved, so probably not."

"It was a good thing you didn't die in the accident."

"That's a frightening thought." She grimaced. "I would have gone to Hell."

"Maybe that's why God allowed you to leave—to find Him."

"Hmm...leaving religion to find God." She let the thought take root.

"I've heard it said that man's religion is one of the greatest forms of evil."

She frowned. "What do you mean?"

"Think about it. Religion keeps people from believing the truth. God says to come to Him, that Jesus is the way to Heaven. Religion says you can get to Heaven if only you do this and this and that. Well, with God, there is no this and this and that. There's Jesus. That's it. *For whosoever shall call upon the name of the Lord shall be saved.* It's that simple."

"But Jathan and the children probably aren't saved." She frowned.

"Probably not."

"But if I divorce him, what kind of testimony would that be?"

Mark frowned. "What are you proposing, Sarah?"

"I don't know. I'm just so confused. On one hand, I wish I'd never come across Jathan. But on the other, I feel like I have a responsibility to him and our children." She shook her head. "I mean, isn't salvation the most important thing? Can I just walk away and let them keep marching toward Hell?"

"I *think* I see your point."

"Think about it, Mark. Put yourself in Jathan's shoes."

"I wouldn't want to be in his shoes. Or his buggy. I'm rather fond of my truck." He chuckled.

"I'm serious, Mark!"

"I know, I know. I just needed a little comic relief."

"What should I do?"

He pulled her near. "All I know is that I'm not giving you up."

"I'm not leaving." She gazed into the eyes she'd fallen in love with.

"I think I might have an idea."

FIVE

Bishop Wagler rubbed his greying beard as he sat across from Jathan at his kitchen table.

Jathan eyed him warily, awaiting his response.

"I hate to say it, Jathan. But this is your own doing. You're reaping the consequences of your actions."

Jathan frowned. "But my Sarah's alive."

The bishop nodded. "And married to another man—an *Englischer*."

"But she's still *my* wife!"

"*Nee*, Jathan. She hasn't been your *fraa* for ten years."

"I still love Sarah." He hated that tears misted his eyes, especially in front of Bishop Wagler. "Seeing her again..." His mind wandered back to Sarah, sleeping so peacefully on the couch. He'd stared at her face for a whole hour, gently stroking her fine hair, while he should've been out working in the field. It had been wonderful *gut* to have her back in the house. To touch her soft face. It was almost like a dream. A wonderful dream.

"There's nothing you can do now, Jathan. You're too late." The bishop's words pulled him out of his trance.

"Why? Can't I go to the judge? Tell him she was my wife first. I can fight for her."

"And if she doesn't want to come home? Jathan, you know that is not our way." The sternness in Bishop Wagler's voice was clear. "Besides, we don't want the *Englisch* in our business. They'll just cause trouble. I think it may have been a mistake allowing you to marry an *Englisch* woman."

"But she'd become Amish. Sarah loved me. I know she did."

"Perhaps."

"Surely, there's *something* I can do." He hated that he sounded so desperate. But he was, wasn't he?

"You can pray. You know God is the Righteous Judge. Go to Him."

"I've already done that."

"You can always pray more. He never tires of hearing from His children."

"I'm afraid God isn't listening. I've been praying for Sarah to come back for ten years now."

Bishop Wagler's eyes widened. "And she has. It sounds as if *Gott* may be listening after all."

Jathan sipped the tea the bishop's wife had offered him earlier. "But I didn't want her to come back this way. I wanted her to come back home. Back to us."

"God's ways are not our ways."

"What does God want from me?"

"Your obedience. Your trust."

"But how can I get my Sarah back?"

"Jathan." The bishop shook his head. "It is not for us to know these things. You just pray, Jathan. Pray for *Der Herr's* will."

Just pray. Jathan thought on the bishop's words as he slapped the reins to urge Driver on. "God, aren't You tired of me praying the same thing by now?" He spoke the words to the air. "I know I am," he mumbled.

"How long, God? How long will my past chase me? I gave up drinking. You know I did. Why, then? Why can't I have my wife back?" *Pray for God's will.* "Okay, God. I'm praying for Your will, but if I could please find favor in Your eyes, I'll do my best to love her like I'm supposed to."

Jathan pulled into the long lane at the edge of his property. Something seemed different—something felt different. He looked toward the house. A charcoal-gray truck was parked in front of the house.

His heart jumped within his chest. Could it be Sarah?

"Yah!" he commanded his mare. He rolled to a stop just in front of the barn. It seemed like it took two weeks just to reach the hitching post.

He slid down, not bothering to tether the horse, and hurried toward the porch.

"Sarah?" he called out, marching up the steps.

"I'm here, Jathan," her delightful voice sounded from the side porch.

Excitement filled his heart. He rounded the corner. And then came to an abrupt stop. His eyes moved to Sarah's side.

"Jathan, I'd like you to meet my husband, Mark." Sarah wore an unsure expression.

Jathan swallowed, and stared at the man's outstretched hand. There was no way he was shaking the hand of the man who stole his wife.

"Nice place you got here," the man said. He dropped his hand to his side.

Jathan frowned. He looked at Sarah. "Why did you bring him with you?"

"I wanted you two to meet."

"Why?"

"Well, because. I wanted you to believe that I *really* am married."

"You're married to me."

"I realize that." Sarah stared at her hands.

"You do?" Well, at least she admitted it now. That was certainly a step in the right direction.

"Yes. I have amnesia."

"Amnesia? What is this?"

"It means that I lost my memory."

Jathan frowned, attempting to take it all in.

The man with Sarah stepped forward. It was apparent he'd rather not be there. "Listen, Jathan. We're trying to make the best out of an awkward situation here. Sarah and I talked and agreed she could stop by once a week to spend time with the children. Are you okay with this arrangement?"

"I want my wife back!" Jathan clenched his hands at his sides.

"I'm sorry, but that's not possible."

Who did this guy think he was? "Sarah, what do *you* say?" His gaze steadied on her.

"I can't come back to you, Jathan. I'm sorry. I have another life now." She reached out and briefly touched his hand. Her eyes searched his. "Would it be better for you if we got a divorce?"

"You would *divorce* me?" Pain gripped his heart at the idea that Sarah would even suggest it.

"If it would make it easier for you. I mean, you could remarry someone else."

He shook his head vigorously. "Never. We do not believe in divorce; God hates it. Even if I could remarry, I don't want to. You're the only woman I've ever wanted. I need *you*, Sarah." How could he convince her to stay and give him a second chance?

The man beside Sarah sighed, clearly becoming impatient. "Will you allow Sarah to see the children once a week, or not?"

Jathan's brow rose. Seeing Sarah once a week was better than not seeing her at all. He would take the crumbs. Maybe he could win her love again. "You would allow her to come?"

"For the *children*, yes," the man said.

"Will *you* come too?" Jathan frowned.

The man glanced at Sarah. "Sarah and I haven't discussed that yet."

"Sarah can come." He smiled at his wife. "She is welcome any time."

Sarah stepped forward. "When would be a good time?"

"Sunday after meeting would be best." He always looked his best on church days. Should he invite her to attend? "We have meeting every two weeks. You...you could come, Sarah." He would ignore the whispers that would no doubt arise from the women at meeting. Who knew what rumors were already flying around the community?

She blessed Jathan with a soft smile, one he hadn't seen in entirely too long. "Thank you for the offer, Jathan. We already have a church that we attend on Sundays."

Jathan then watched as his wife drove away with another man. If only he could go back and do things differently. If only he could win her devotion again.

SIX

Mark pulled the vehicle up to the house. Their girls hopped out and scurried to the front door in their Sunday best, waiting patiently.

He turned to Sarah before exiting the vehicle. "Are you sure you want to do this?"

She sighed. "I feel like I *need* to do this. I'm their mother."

"It's not your girls that have me concerned; it's him. I don't trust him."

She rubbed his hand. "Jathan does still love me, that's true. But what can I do? It's not like we're ever going to have a romantic relationship again. *This* is my home. *You* are the one I kiss goodnight."

Mark nodded. "I know. I trust you. I just...maybe I should go with you."

"I appreciate it, but that's not necessary. Just enjoy

your day off with the girls, yeah? And don't worry, I'll be fine."

The girls knocked on the window, their patience gone. Mark opened the door. "I'm coming, I'm coming!"

The girls looked to Sarah. "What about Mommy?"

Sarah smiled. "Mommy's going to go visit someone today."

Mark chimed in, "Yep, and if you two are really good, we'll get pizza for dinner!" He looked back and winked at Sarah.

"Hooray!"

Sarah smiled at their daughters' enthusiasm and waved as the three of them walked to the front door, away from her car. Mark blew her a kiss, which she promptly caught and returned. She moved to the driver's seat and briefly sent up a prayer for both of her families.

How was this ever going to work out?

Sarah hadn't anticipated all of the Sunday traffic in Amish Country. The usual one-and-a-half-hour drive took nearly two, which meant she'd have less time with the girls than expected. She glanced inside each buggy as she passed them one by one, thinking that

Jathan and the girls might occupy one. No such luck.

She thought that surely Jathan and the girls would be at the house by the time she arrived, but they weren't. Sarah took her time while she roamed around the property. No memories stirred.

Perhaps it was a good thing she didn't remember. God only knew what those lost memories held.

Mom had said that Jathan wasn't a good man and that she'd left him. Seeing Jathan now, he didn't seem like the type of man that would have a problem with anger. His—or their, rather—girls didn't seem to be overtly afraid of him, so she didn't see him as the abusive type. What had Mom meant?

The clip-clop of horse hooves and the rattle of buggy wheels beckoned her out of the garden. Jathan's face lit up when their eyes briefly met. He said a few words in Pennsylvania Dutch and the two oldest girls scurried to the house—but not until after acknowledging her presence with steady eyes. What did the girls think of all this?

The three younger girls followed the oldest two and Jathan gestured Sarah near. She hesitantly obliged, remembering Mark's words of caution before she'd left Baltimore.

Jathan's unapologetic stare made her uncomfortable. He cleared his throat. "The girls don't know that you have another family. They think you've been away because you've been sick."

Her jaw dropped.

"I had to tell them something when you left. They think God brought their *Mamm* back to them, answered their prayers."

"Jathan, you know I can't stay. Why didn't you tell them?"

"They've had it hard enough with you gone. I wouldn't know what to say. Do I just tell them that their *mamm* abandoned them and found a new family to love?"

Tears welled in her eyes. "How about the truth?"

"Which is?"

Did *she* even know the truth?

"I don't know! My mother said I left because you weren't a good man. *You* even said you had a problem with drinking." She wiped a tear from her cheek. "All I know is that I was in a really bad car accident when I was twenty-five. I woke up in a hospital room with both of my parents at my side. You weren't there. Nobody from the Amish community was there. My parents took me home and I lived with them until Mark and I married. Nobody told me I'd ever had an Amish family, that I was a wife and mother."

"You mean, your folks didn't say nothing to you?"

"Not a word." She shook her head. "And the accident wiped out my memory."

"You *really* don't know me?"

"That's what I've been trying to tell you this whole time, Jathan. You are a complete stranger, as far as I'm concerned."

He frowned and shook his head. "I guess your folks never did like me none."

"What do you mean?"

"Well, when we—" Jathan was cut off by one of the girls calling for dinner. "I guess we'd better go in. We can talk later."

Sarah nodded. As they entered the house, she couldn't stop thinking about Jathan's words—*Your folks never did like me.* Had they deliberately neglected to tell her about her past just to keep her and Jathan apart because they didn't *like* him? *Unbelievable!*

Jathan pulled out a chair for Sarah to sit in. She watched as the oldest girl dished out soup for each person.

"Thank you." She would have said the girl's name but she didn't know what it was. What kind of a mother doesn't know her own daughter's name? She looked to Jathan for help.

"Sarah, do we have any bread to go with this?" His eyes stayed on the oldest girl, then he glanced back at her.

So they'd named their daughter after *her*?

"*Nee*, Da. We used up the last of it for breakfast. I'll make more on Tuesday."

Sarah began, "It's been so long since I—"

"Mary, Anna, Becky, Julie." Jathan abruptly cut her off. Was he afraid that she might say something to hurt the girls? "You girls help Sarah clean up after the meal. *Mamm* and I need to talk some."

Sarah closed her mouth and just enjoyed the meal. She was sure to tell Sarah and the other girls, whose names she tried hard to remember, that they'd done a good job in preparing it. This brought huge, yet demure smiles to their faces. She wondered if Jathan complimented them often. It appeared Jathan had done a good job raising them alone.

SEVEN

"I should help the girls," Sarah protested as Jathan beckoned her out to the porch.

"*Nee*, they're used to cleaning up. Come, we should talk."

Sarah sat on the rugged porch swing and Jathan plopped down by her side.

He blew out a breath. "What do you want to know about the past?"

Sarah shrugged, a gentle smile tugged at her lips. "Everything?"

Jathan chuckled. "I don't think you're planning on spending the night, no?"

She shook her head.

"Well, I guess I'll start with when we met." Jathan's countenance brightened. "You were on roller skates."

"Roller skates?"

"*Jah*." He smiled. "There used to be a restaurant in

town where folks drove up and flashed their lights."

"I was a car hop?" Sarah raised a brow. "That sounds like fun."

"I think that may be what the *Englisch* called it. Anyway, Pete Yoder and I decided to stop there one day for supper. I heard they had good hamburgers."

"Did they?"

"*Jah*. Anyhow, when you rolled up to my buggy, you asked what we wanted." He gave a sheepish smile. "I said I'd like a date with you."

Sarah's mouth hung open. "You didn't!"

"*Jah*, I did."

"What'd I say?"

"No."

Her eyes widened. "No?" She laughed.

"I guess you already had a beau."

"I did? Who?" Not that she would know the person anyway.

"Don't know, and at that time I didn't care." He shrugged. "I came back every week just to see if you still had a beau. Every week, I asked you for a date."

"You were bold."

"*Jah, vell*, when you know what you want..." He shook his head. "One day, you said yes. After that, we started courting. No one in my district knew for a while. They don't want Amish and *Englisch* to mix, you know."

"How old were we?"

"I think you were seventeen. I was eighteen already."

Sarah shook her head, attempting to picture the scene in her mind.

"I knew right away I wanted to marry you. Bishop said no, but I kept begging him. Every other week at meeting, I'd ask him. Finally, after several months, I think he realized I wasn't gonna give up." Jathan laughed.

"You're a persistent one."

"For sure and certain. He said if you had in mind to become Amish that he wouldn't be against it. But you had to learn *Deitsch* and follow our ways."

"And I did?"

"*Jah*. You done real *gut*. But your folks..." Jathan shook his head. "When they found out that we were thinking about getting hitched, they came unglued. Your folks forbade you to see me."

"Why?"

"Guess they didn't want you joining our people. Or maybe they didn't like me none. I don't know for sure." He scratched his beard. "You know, it wonders me how your folks could dislike me so much, seeing that they never even wanted to meet me."

"So, are you saying my parents never even met you?" Sarah frowned at Jathan's nod. "How did we end up married?"

"We didn't tell your folks. The day we got hitched, you left the house after your folks went to work. You were almost nineteen by then. It was on a Tuesday, so I don't think they suspected anything. When you didn't show up at home, they came looking for you. It was the next morning when your *vatter* showed up, but he was too late."

"Less than a year later, we had little Sarah." Jathan smiled. "You were such a *gut mamm*."

Heat rose in her cheeks. "So, what about the drinking?"

Jathan's Adam's apple bobbed. "Something I wish I could go back and redo." Tears misted in his eyes. "I swear, Sarah. If I could only go back and change it."

"But you can't."

"*Nee.*" He quickly shoved a hand to his face, removing the tear that had been there a second before. "I was working. It was at a frolic."

"A frolic?"

He nodded. "We were putting up a new barn for Pete's dad. I fell and hurt my leg perty bad. We had some whiskey. For pain, you know. I start drinking it and it helped a lot. But my leg. I couldn't go back to work. Our bills started piling up and we couldn't pay 'em. You didn't know at first. I shoulda told you. Instead, I drank away my worry." He shook his head. "Anyway, when you found out, you were upset. I shoulda been out working. We had babies to feed and here I was spending what little we had on alcohol. You begged me to stop, but I didn't. You told me you were gonna leave if I didn't stop. I didn't think you really would. Until you did."

Sarah couldn't help her tears.

"Like I said, the drinking stopped that day. I knew that if I didn't, I'd never get you back and I'd probably lose the girls too. I went back to work when the girls were at school. When they went to bed at night, I'd go out searching for you. I thought that if you knew that I quit drinking and got a job, you'd come back home. But I never did find you. Not till now."

"Jathan..." Sarah's breath came in shallow puffs. "I don't know what to say."

"I'd give anything for you to stay with us, Sarah. Anything."

"I can't, Jathan."

Sarah easily read the regret in his eyes, heard it in his tone. "I don't understand. Why would your folks do that to us? They knew we were hitched."

She lifted her hands. "I don't know. You said they didn't want us to be together."

"I think they hated me after I married you. They didn't even know about our *bopplin*."

"*Bopplin*?"

"Our babies." Jathan cracked his knuckles. "Never cared to visit once. In fact, I think they moved away."

"They moved away? But I thought..." *Had they lied about that too?*

"You lived in Gordonville."

"Wow. And I thought my parents were good people. How could they lie to me about all these things? What I've thought was my past life is really just a bunch of lies."

He stood up from the porch swing and paced. "What I don't understand is how *they* found out about your accident, but I had no idea."

"My mom said I had my old driver's license in my wallet. I guess I had no Amish identification and I was most likely wearing regular clothes. The police probably had no indication that I'd been Amish. Otherwise, they likely would have contacted the Amish community."

"When was your accident?"

"August fourth. But I was in a coma for a couple of weeks, they said."

"Just two days after you left." Frustration clenched his hands.

The creaking of the screen door drew their attention.

Sarah rose from the swing. "I should probably get to know the girls some while I'm here. What do you want me to tell them?"

EIGHT

Jathan spoke several strings of sentences in Pennsylvania Dutch to the girls, which Sarah couldn't decipher.

Their gazes somber, each of the girls nodded and gave Sarah a hug, and she breathed in the faint lingering scent of their shampoo.

Sarah and Jathan walked to her car and Sarah gestured toward the house. "What did you say to the girls in there?"

"I said their *mamm* had to go away for a while, but she'd be back again next week."

"What did Anna say to you?"

"She asked why Momma wasn't staying here with them. She asked why Momma don't love them no more."

Sarah couldn't help it when the moisture gathered in her eyes. "Jathan, I don't know if I can do this.

Those girls need a mother and I can't be one to them."

Jathan placed his hands on Sarah's shoulders, his emphatic gaze penetrating hers. "Sarah, you're their mother whether you like it or not. You're the only one they got. They need *you*. They need *your* love. And although you may not remember them, they remember their momma that loved them and raised them."

"I just feel so torn. How can I make this work?"

"I can't tell you that, Sarah. But what I can tell you is that you have a family here that loves you."

She sighed and moved to the driver's side door. "I have *two* families that love me." That should be a blessing, right? So, then why did it feel like a curse?

She pulled the car door open to get in.

"Sarah?"

She looked up. "Yeah?"

Jathan's hand rested over hers on the door's frame. "We're really glad you came."

"Thanks, Jathan." She removed her hand. "Thank you for telling me about our past."

Sarah closed the door and started the engine. She waved to Jathan and the girls, who now stood on the front porch watching her vehicle exit their driveway.

For some reason, she hadn't thought leaving would be this hard. But with each mile that separated them, it seemed like the gulf in her heart became that much wider.

She pondered Jathan's story about how they'd met, and tried to picture Jathan as a clean-shaven younger man. She admitted to herself that she found Jathan attractive, even with his facial hair. His eyes were stunning, actually. *Is that wrong, Lord? He* is *my husband, after all.*

But then, so was Mark. How would *he* feel if he could read her thoughts?

She banged the steering wheel in frustration. How did a person get into this type of conundrum? *God, why is this happening? And how on earth am I supposed to fix it?*

She waited in silence as though her words would receive an audible answer. Nothing.

If only there was a way to know what the right thing to do was. If only God would say, "*This is the way, walk ye in it,*" as he had to the Children of Israel.

"How did your time with the girls go?" Mark's smile brought a small measure of comfort amidst Sarah's dueling thoughts.

"Okay." Her eyes roamed the living room. "Where are Brooke and Claire?"

"They were tired, so I put them to bed." He gestured toward the girls' room. "What do you mean by just okay?"

"It's kind of complicated." She fell into their leather sofa and kicked off her shoes.

"How so?"

"Well, it turns out that Jathan told them I've been sick. They think I'm eventually returning to them to be their mother."

"Why in the world would he tell them that? He knows you're not coming back for good." Mark joined Sarah on the couch.

"I'm not too sure about that."

"He thinks you *are* coming back?" Mark frowned. "You set him straight though, right?"

"Yes. I told him that I can only come back to visit the girls."

"Maybe I should go with you next time."

Sarah grimaced. "I don't know if that's such a good idea."

"Why not?"

"Well, Jathan said the girls don't know that I have another family."

"What?"

"He hasn't told them." She hiked her aching feet onto the ottoman.

"I can't believe this. Did *you* tell them?"

"Jathan asked me not to."

"And you complied?" The disappointment in Mark's tone was clear.

"Mark, this is a very delicate situation. They're my children. And Jathan's. I just... I don't want to reemerge out of the blue and then drop a bombshell on them. I'm going to let Jathan break the news to them when he feels the time is right."

"I don't get it. Why not just tell them the truth?"

"Well, how about our girls? They don't know the truth of this situation either."

"I guess you have a point."

"This is a difficult situation for everyone involved." Sarah shook her head. "I'm so frustrated with my parents right now, I can't even begin to..." She wanted to scream.

"I don't know why your parents did what they did, but I'm sure they had your best interests in mind."

"I don't think so. I think their reasons were purely selfish."

"Why do you say that?"

"Jathan said that they never did approve of him and me being together. Because of that, we married without their blessing. Before the accident, I hadn't seen them for years, and they've never even seen

Jathan's and my children. What kind of parents do that?"

"Did they know you had children?"

"Jathan said they moved away after they found out we'd gotten married. They'd all but disowned me."

"What if Jathan's lying?"

"I don't think so."

"Are you going to talk to your parents?"

"You bet I am."

"But does it really matter now? I mean, you can't go back and change the past."

"No, but they should know how I feel. And they should know that they have Amish grandchildren."

"What do you think they'll do?"

"They probably won't even care. Why would they?"

"Man, I've always liked your parents. I hate to think of them as evil masterminds." He shook his head. "You think you know someone."

"I never thought my parents could be capable of something so deceitful. I'm just baffled as to why they'd do that. I mean, how do they think their behavior is justified? Do they think it's okay just to step in and play God and ruin other people's lives?"

Hurt crossed Mark's features. "Is that how you feel, Sarah? Like your life's been ruined?"

"No, that's not what I meant."

"Really? Because it almost sounds like you regret marrying me and having our children."

Sarah attempted to remain calm. "Mark, I don't regret you or our children."

"But if you could go back, you'd still be Amish."

"I didn't say that."

"What are you saying then, Sarah?"

"I'm saying that all this could have been prevented."

"Prevented?" His voice rose. "Are you serious?"

This added stress wasn't doing anything to help her impending headache. "No, Mark, you're not understanding me."

"No, I think I am."

"Don't be ridiculous! You know I love you and the girls."

He stood from the sofa and crossed his arms over his chest. "Then put an end to your ties with your other family."

"What?"

"You heard me."

"I can't do that." Sarah stared at Mark as though he'd arrived from another planet. "You can't ask me to just cut ties with my own flesh and blood. That's not fair, Mark."

"You said you loved us. I'm asking you to prove it.

Sarah, those people are strangers to you. You don't even know them. It would be easy to walk away right now."

Never mind the fact that she loved her *other* family too. "So, what? This is an ultimatum?"

"If that's what you want to call it."

"So, I leave them or...what?" *Is he really doing this?*

"I'm not sharing you. You're *my* wife! And the mother of our girls."

"Mark, you're going to wake the girls," she warned, attempting to bring the conversation volume down a notch or two.

"I don't care."

"It's once a week."

"For now. And then what?"

"This was *your* idea, Mark. And I think it was a good one."

"I don't."

"I think *my* children have a right to know their mother. I'm sorry that you have to get dragged into all of this, but it's our reality now. The least you can do is be understanding and supportive."

"I just have this ominous feeling. Like I'm going to lose you."

"I'm not going anywhere," she assured.

Mark sighed and pulled Sarah into his arms. "You

sure about that?" He kissed the top of her head, but his voice was fraught with doubt.

"Yes."

"I think we should go talk to Pastor."

Sarah shook her head. "I don't want to."

"Why not?"

"He advised me to divorce Jathan."

"And that's a bad thing?" Mark pulled back from their embrace.

"God hates divorce. How can a minister of God advise me to do something that is an abomination to Him?"

"Sometimes it's necessary."

"Would you be saying the same thing if you were in Jathan's shoes?"

"Will you *please* stop saying *his* name, Sarah?"

"I didn't realize it bothered you," she said quietly.

"Wouldn't it bother *you* if you discovered *I* was married to someone else and talked about her all the time?"

"I don't talk about Jath...about *him* all the time."

"It seems like that's *all* we've discussed since you discovered your past."

Sarah blew out a frustrated breath. "Okay, then let's just not talk about it."

"Fine."

"Come. Sit." She patted the cushion next to her, hoping to disarm her husband's defenses. "How were the girls tonight?"

"Other than missing their mother, they were fine. We watched a Bible cartoon." Mark sat down and sighed.

"Oh, yeah? Which one?"

"I think the one about Zacchaeus."

"Oh, they love that one. I think it's their favorite." She smiled.

"I crack up every time Caiaphas talks."

"Yeah. They sure did give him an interesting character." She smiled. "Did you get pizza?"

"Of course."

Sarah glanced up at the clock. Was it really that late? "We should get to bed. You've got to get up early for work tomorrow."

"Yeah, you're right." Mark's eyes darted to his watch. "Whoa, is it really eleven?"

"Yep."

"It would probably be better if you came home a little earlier next time."

Sarah wanted to protest. She wanted to tell Mark that Jathan's girls only got to see their mother for a few hours, and only once out of an entire week. But she'd bite her tongue. This time, anyway.

"Come, my beautiful wife." Mark smiled. "Let us take our fill of love till morning," he winked, quoting Solomon.

"And I thought you wanted sleep." She chuckled and raised a brow.

"Yeah, I'll take some of that too."

NINE

"**M**ark?"

Mark looked up from the document he was working on. Interruptions while he was working were not welcome. The distractions caused him to lose his focus. But when it was from his boss, well, it really couldn't be ignored. "What do you need, Ted?"

"I have a proposition for you."

"I'm listening." He leaned back in his chair with his hands clasped behind his head.

"You've been with our company for a long time. We like you. You've been a great worker. You've shown integrity and I admire your leadership skills. I guess what I'm saying is, we'd like to give you a promotion." His boss smiled. "Interested?"

"In a promotion? I'd be a fool not to be. What does it in involve?"

"Here's the catch." Ted sat on the edge of Mark's desk and twirled a pencil between his fingers. "It's in Maine."

"Maine?" Mark leaned forward and frowned.

Ted held up a hand. "Don't dismiss the idea yet. Just hear me out. The company will pay for you to relocate. Which means, as long as you're with our company, we're paying your mortgage. The majority of the work will be from home, so you'll only need to go into the office once or twice a week. Oh yeah, and did I mention the pay is great?"

"Ah, Ted, that sounds like a dream." A million visions swam through Mark's head. More time at home with Sarah and the girls. More money to do whatever.

"Think about it. The position will be open for you until the end of the month. After that, I'll have to offer it to someone else. I'd really like to see you advance in this company. You deserve it, Mark."

Mark nodded. "Okay, I'll talk to my wife about it. Thanks, Ted."

"Don't thank me. I'm gonna hate to lose you, to tell the truth." His boss nodded and closed the door, disappearing from Mark's sight.

Maine. If there ever was an opportunity to save his family, this was it.

Sarah stared at the coffee mug she held in her hands. This was usually one of her favorite times of the day. She'd just walked the girls to their bus stop and saw them off to school. Mark had left a couple of hours earlier. This was her quiet time. Just her, a cup of coffee, and God.

She flipped open her Bible and continued where she'd left off. She'd already searched every verse she could on divorce, but the simple answer remained elusive. None of the verses were applicable to her situation.

If Pastor Joe had a chapter and verse to show where his recommendation came from, she'd be satisfied. There would be no question as to what was right and wrong. But the question still remained, and there were too many lives at stake to get this wrong.

She couldn't shake the feeling she'd had last night while lying in Mark's arms. She'd felt...*guilty*? Or was that even the proper word for it? Uneasy, for sure. Like she was cheating on Jathan. Yet, she and Mark were married.

Sarah felt like beating her head against the wall. How was she ever going to sort out this confusion? God was not the author of confusion, she knew that much, but why had God allowed these circumstances in her life? What was the purpose? And how in the world was she supposed to find the answer?

The sound of her cell phone vibrating drew her attention to her purse on the counter. She sighed and rose from the table. Upon glancing at the number, she realized it was most likely a telemarketer—the last thing she wanted to deal with in her overly complicated life. She quickly pushed the "decline" option and returned to her attempted Bible study. The phone rang again just as she sat down.

"Hello?" At least if she answered, she could press number four to be put on the do-not-call list.

"Sarah?" a male voice asked.

"Yes. Who's calling?"

"It's Jathan, your husband." *Husband.*

"Jathan, I gave you this number for emergencies. You really shouldn't be—"

"It's our Sarah Joy! She was cleaning a window outside the attic. She fell—a long way down. She's in the hospital. Hurt real bad." His distraught voice frightened her.

"When? How long ago?"

"About an hour ago."

"Oh, no. Where is she, Jathan? Which hospital?"

"Lancaster."

"Okay, I'll be there as soon as I can." Sarah quickly ended the call.

Dear God, please let my Sarah be all right.

She frantically scribbled a note for Mark, then headed out the door. She raced toward Lancaster, pushing the speed limits more than she normally would. Sarah prayed the entire trip, which caused the drive to seem a lot shorter than it was in actuality.

When Sarah entered the hospital, she immediately noticed Amish people walking toward the waiting room. Were they here for her Sarah or were they visiting another patient? She looked to see if any of them might be Jathan. They were not.

A quick survey of the waiting room told her Jathan was not in there either.

"Sarah?" A woman's voice called from the waiting room just as she was exiting.

Sarah turned around to see a woman near her own age walking toward her. Her burgundy cape dress and prayer *kapp* identified her as Amish. "Yes?"

The woman didn't look familiar, but that meant little where Sarah was concerned. There was a time in her life when she knew no one at all, not even her parents. It had been a very dark time after the accident. Every piece of her past had been reconstructed for her. She'd trusted her parents to tell her the truth. Now she wondered just how much could be believed of what they'd told her.

"I'm Ruth. Jathan's sister."

Sarah nodded. "Do you know which room Sarah Joy is in?"

"*Jah*, I can show you which way, but I'm not allowed to go in. Only her *vatter* and *mudder* can go in."

Sarah followed her sister-in-law to a set of double doors.

"She's in ICU. You'll have to ask for her at the desk."

"Okay. Thank you, Ruth."

Sarah took a deep breath and stepped through the double doors, leaving her sister-in-law behind. After a nurse pointed her to the correct door number, she gingerly stepped into the hospital room where her daughter lay injured.

Sarah Joy, whom Jathan had said was now sixteen and out of school, lay with her long hair about her shoulders. Her prayer *kapp* was cast aside on a small bedside table and she still wore her Amish clothing. An uncomfortable-looking plastic neck brace prohibited her from much movement, although she now slept.

Sarah's eyes moved to Jathan, who sat with his head in his hands. He obviously hadn't heard her enter the room. She briefly deliberated calling his name out.

No, she wouldn't interrupt his prayers.

She quietly walked toward Sarah Joy's bedside. This was her daughter. A daughter that she'd already lost too much time with, thanks to her parents' deceit. Now, it seemed her time with her daughter could be cut even shorter. What if she didn't make it through this?

"Sarah?" Jathan called out in a hoarse whisper.

She looked to Jathan, who seemed weary. His eyes brimmed with tears and Sarah quickly planted herself next to him.

"They said she might not make it," his voice trembled.

Sarah couldn't help but offer Jathan the comfort he needed—the comfort they *both* needed. When Jathan released her from his embrace, she felt strengthened. There was an unspoken communion between them as they sat weeping and silently praying together for nearly ten minutes.

"Has she been asleep the whole time?" Sarah's eyes wandered over her daughter's still body.

"*Jah.*" He took Sarah's hand in his. "She asked about you yester night after you left. She was glad you came, but she said you were different from how she remembered you. I asked her how. She said you didn't know her or her *schweschdern*. I explained to her that you were in an accident and couldn't remember nothing."

Sarah nodded, mentally correcting his grammar.

"She said she wished she could know you, like her cousins know their *mamms*. She said she wished you could stay with us forever." His eyes met hers.

"What did you tell her?" Sarah swallowed.

"I said I wished you could too."

Sarah couldn't hold back any longer. She broke down. Her shoulders convulsed with sobs, and Jathan's strong arm pulled her close. "I'm so sorry, Jathan. This is so hard. I don't know what to do."

"You're doing it now, Sarah. You're here." He whispered in hushed tones. "That's what she needs now. She needs her *mamm* here."

When she was able to gather her emotions, she looked up at Jathan. "I don't know how you do it."

"Do what?"

"You're so calm. I'm a mess, and you're *calm*."

He shrugged. "Guess I've always been that way. Maybe that's why God saw fit to put us together. I don't know."

Sarah followed his gaze, which went to Sarah Joy. "What? What is it?"

"I think I saw her fingers move a bit."

"Was that the first time?"

He nodded. "Since we been here, *jah*. She's just been sleeping."

Sarah stared at their daughter, willing her fingers to move again. *Nothing.* "Should we tell the nurse?"

He shook his head. "They said to get them if she wakes up."

"Maybe I should talk to her."

"I guess it wouldn't hurt none."

Sarah walked to her daughter's bedside. "Sarah, honey, it's Momma. Dad is here too." She glanced at Jathan. "We'll be here when you're ready to wake up. We...we can talk. I know we didn't get much time yesterday because I had to go. I wish I could have stayed longer." She felt like she was babbling, but Jathan urged her on. "I know you haven't seen much of me over the years, but I hope to change that. You see, I was in an accident. When I woke up, I didn't remember who I was."

Jathan reached over and touched her hand. He shook his head.

"You don't want me to tell her?" she whispered.

"Not too much."

"Okay." She turned back to Sarah Joy. "I'll be here, Sarah. I'm not going anywhere."

Jathan lightly clenched her arm and she turned toward him.

Her eyes narrowed. "What?"

"Don't give her false hope. Don't say you're staying unless you mean it." His tone was firm.

"I plan to stay here, at least until she wakes up."

Jathan frowned and beckoned her to the opposite side of the room. "Do you mean that?" he whispered.

"Yes."

"What about your other family?"

"I left a note for Mark. I'm sure he'll understand. When he calls, I'm going to explain things to him. My mother can watch the girls if I need her to."

Doubt creased his brow. "Your *mamm?*" Jathan most likely despised her parents for showing her and Mark's children preferential treatment. How could they treat Brooke and Claire like princesses when they hadn't even made an effort to meet her and Jathan's girls? It all seemed so unjust.

"Yes, Mark will see that they're taken care of."

"You're sure?"

"Well, he may not be pleased, but Sarah needs me now."

"Then I'll stay too."

"Were you planning to leave?"

"Well, I was gonna go home to check on the girls and milk the goats, but I can have John do it."

"John?"

"My sister Ruth's husband. They *chust* live down the road a bit. I'll have Ruth check on the girls."

Sarah's eyes widened. "They're home alone?"

"Yep, they're used to it."

Sarah's head spun. *The girls were home? All alone?* She stared at Jathan, attempting to comprehend the situation. "Mary is what, fifteen?"

"Fourteen. And plenty capable of running a house."

Hadn't she just read an article about some lunatic breaking into someone's house and kidnapping two teenage girls?

"*Der Herr*—God—is with them," Jathan assured.

Sarah breathed a sigh of relief. Yes, their girls weren't little like Claire and Brooke. And they were Amish and lived in Amish Country. Amish Country was safer, wasn't it?

"I'll go talk to Ruth." He glanced at Sarah Joy, then back to her. "You'll stay here?"

"Yes. I'm not going anywhere." Sarah lifted a half-smile.

Jathan nodded, and she watched as he left the room.

She ambled over to Sarah Joy's bedside. She grasped her eldest daughter's hand. "Oh, how I wish I could have more time to get to know you, Sarah Joy."

"Momma?"

Sarah startled at the voice and her eyes darted to her daughter's face. "Sarah Joy, you're awake?"

"*Jah*, Momma."

"Don't move, honey. You should lie as still as possible." She should run to get the nurse, but she didn't want to leave Sarah Joy here alone. It could wait till Jathan returned, couldn't it?

"How are you feeling, sweetheart?"

"Okay. A little tired." Her eyes grazed the room. "Is Simon here?"

"Simon?"

"My beau."

Sarah's eyebrow shot up. "You—you're sixteen. You have a boyfriend?"

"Simon and I have been courting for six months. We'll probably marry next year." She looked around again. "Is *Dat* here?"

"Yes, he's talking to your Aunt Ruth."

"Water?" Her voice sounded hoarse.

Sarah grasped the pitcher on the bedside table and poured some water into the empty cup that accompanied it. She placed a straw in it and brought it to Sarah Joy's lips.

"That's better." She smiled. "I miss you, Momma."

"I miss you too, Sarah Joy."

"Why won't you come home to live with us?"

"It's complicated." She knew that wasn't a good explanation, but she was unsure what exactly Jathan wanted her to share. "I live in Baltimore now."

"Do you still love *Dat?*"

It was an honest question and one that demanded an answer. "I, uh—"

"Sarah Joy? You're awake?" Jathan's excited voice called from behind her.

Had he heard their daughter's question?

"Yes, she is." Sarah smiled, relieved to not have to answer Sarah Joy. "I'll go get the doctor now that you're here. I didn't want to leave her."

Jathan nodded. Pleasure clearly marked his features.

"How are you feeling?" Sarah heard Jathan ask their daughter, as she walked out.

She hastened to the nurses station and informed the nurse on duty of Sarah Joy's status.

"I'll send someone in." The older woman smiled. "Are you her mother?"

"Yes, I am."

"You must be pleased."

Sarah nodded. "Her father and I are both very happy."

"Jathan's your husband?"

"Yes."

The nurse frowned, and a confused expression crossed her face. "You're not Amish?"

"Uh, no."

"I'm sorry. It's none of my business, really. I've just never seen an Amish man with an Amish daughter, who has a wife who isn't Amish."

"Our situation is a little different." Sarah looked back toward her daughter's room where a doctor was now entering. "I really should go back in there."

"Oh, yes. Of course."

Sarah never imagined being in such an awkward situation. The lady probably thought they were crazy. In fact, *she'd* probably think it was crazy if it were someone else in the same predicament. But, no, this reality with all its absurdities, belonged to her. And strangely enough, she was beginning to get used to it.

She'd almost made it to the door, when the nurse touched her arm. "Ma'am, there's someone in the waiting room for you. He says *he's* your *husband?*"

Sarah forced a smile. *Yep, this woman definitely thinks I'm crazy now. Either that or she thinks I'm in some polygamist cult.* She wasn't about to explain it.

"Could you tell him I'll be out there in just a little while, please? I want to check on my daughter first."

"Sure thing, sugar."

What is Mark doing here?

Sarah sighed and walked back into her daughter's hospital room. Jathan stood quietly by the door and Sarah noticed that the curtain around the bed was drawn.

"What's going on?"

"Doctor's checking her." Jathan's sober countenance made Sarah realize his concern.

"Is he worried?"

"Don't know."

"Will he be long? Mark's here."

Jathan frowned. "Go to him."

Sarah nodded. "I'll be back."

"You can go home now." Jathan's voice was stern.

"No, I want to stay here with Sarah Joy. I'll be back."

Jathan nodded, but Sarah didn't miss the relieved look that briefly flashed across his features.

She made her way down the hallway and back through the double doors. Mark stood just outside the waiting room.

"Sarah. I came as soon as I could." Mark rushed to embrace her.

"You didn't have to."

"I realize that. I just thought maybe you could use some moral support."

"Thanks, honey. I really appreciate it. That was thoughtful of you."

"How is she?"

Sarah shrugged. "Well, she just woke up, so I think that's a good thing. Her neck is in a brace, but I'm unsure of her injuries. Jathan and the doctor are with her now, so we should know soon."

"Jathan was in there with you?"

"Well, yeah. Of course."

He threw his hands in the air. "Of course."

"We're her parents, Mark."

"Yeah, I know. I'm sorry. It's just that thinking of you alone in a room with him drives me crazy."

"We weren't alone, Sarah was there."

"But you said she was asleep."

"That's true." Sarah sighed. "What do you want me to do, Mark?"

"Come home."

"I can't do that. I told Sarah Joy I'd stay here with her."

Mark frowned. "Is he staying too?"

"I don't know."

"Well, that's just great."

"Mark, she's my daughter. I love her just as much as Brooke and Claire."

"How can you say that? You barely even know these people."

Sarah stared at Mark, dumbfounded. Until this moment, she hadn't realized how selfish Mark could be. Did he really only care about his own wants? Was there no empathy in the depths of his soul for her other children?

The painful thought clenched her heart.

TEN

Sarah stood in disbelief as she watched Mark march toward his truck. Did he *really* expect her to leave her daughter here at the hospital and just go on with life? As though she didn't even exist? He'd never suggest such a thing if it were Brooke or Claire. Never.

"Sarah, the doctor would like to speak with both of us," Jathan's voice beckoned her as she stood watching Mark's truck now pull out of the hospital parking lot.

She hastily wiped away a frustrated tear, so Jathan wouldn't think something was wrong.

"I'm coming." She turned an about-face and headed toward Sarah Joy's room with Jathan at her side.

"Mark left already?"

"Yes."

"He didn't stay long."

"No."

"Did he want you to leave with him?"

"Yes."

"But you didn't." She didn't miss the look of pleasure on Jathan's face.

"I told Sarah Joy that I'd stay here with her. I meant it."

"I cannot blame him for wanting you to come home."

A half-smile tipped Sarah's lips. It seemed like Jathan would give just about anything to have her back. The thought both pleased and saddened her. If only there were two of her. But, of course, there weren't.

The doctor greeted them as they approached Sarah Joy's room. "It would probably be best if we spoke out here."

Sarah glanced down the hallway. A nurse walked from one of the other rooms and headed toward the nurses station. Fortunately, nobody else was around to listen in on their conversation.

"Our Sarah Joy will be all right?" Jathan's brow lowered as he asked the doctor.

"I can't give any definitive answers, but your daughter appears to have injured her spinal cord. Sarah Joy most likely will never walk again."

"No, this cannot be!" Jathan's outburst of emotion surprised Sarah.

"I'm sorry." The doctor frowned.

Sarah placed a hand on Jathan's back, attempting to offer comfort. He pulled her into his arms and wept on her shoulder. She would allow him the strength he needed. No doubt, this was more difficult for him than it was for her. Although she loved their daughter too, it was Jathan who'd primarily raised her. He knew her far better than she did.

"Doctor, does Sarah Joy know?" Sarah asked.

"No. I thought it would be best if the two of you were present. I can tell her, or if you'd rather, you may."

Jathan released Sarah from his embrace. "Please tell her for us. You can explain better than we can," he said to the doctor.

Sarah looked steadily at the doctor. "Is there some kind of physical therapy that can help her? Surgery?"

"I'm afraid not, Mrs. Stolzfus."

"Oh, I'm not..." Instead of having to explain their situation to the doctor, Sarah let it go. She glanced at Jathan, who nodded.

"Shall we tell her now?" The doctor looked to both of them.

They nodded in unison.

Jathan led the way into Sarah Joy's hospital room, and Sarah silently prayed their daughter would take the news well.

Sarah Joy's expression turned from one of hope to hopelessness as the doctor explained her condition. "You're saying I...I will never walk again?" She looked to her father and frowned.

"That is correct," the doctor said. "Do you have any questions I can answer?"

Sarah Joy shook her head as best as she could.

The doctor turned to Jathan. "I'll leave you three alone to discuss this amongst yourselves."

Sarah watched as the door closed behind the doctor. *Poor Sarah Joy. What must she be thinking?*

Sarah Joy was quiet. Sarah and Jathan gave her some time to process the news she'd just been given. She looked to her parents. "No man will want to marry me now. No one will want a wife who can't walk—who can't even take care of the children or raise a garden or clean the house!"

"That's not true, Sarah Joy." Sarah tried to sound hopeful.

"It is, Momma! You don't know. You're *Englisch*. It's different in the *Englisch* world. Tell her, *Dat*." Sarah Joy didn't cry, although Sarah knew she must be frustrated.

He reached for Sarah Joy's hand. His sympathetic gesture warmed Sarah's heart. "Sarah Joy, we cannot know the future."

"You know it's true, *Dat*."

"A *gut* man will look past that," he assured her.

"Would you have married Momma if she couldn't walk?" Sarah Joy frowned. "Be honest, *Dat*."

Sarah looked at the floor and pondered her daughter's question.

"Absolutely." He didn't even hesitate. "There's nothing in this world that could've kept me from marrying your Momma."

Unbidden tears pricked Sarah's eyes. She looked at Jathan. "Do you truly mean that?"

He nodded in adamancy.

She briefly wondered if Mark would've said the same thing. *I'm sure he would.*

Sarah looked to her daughter. "Sarah Joy, I know this news is a shock to you right now. If it's alright with your father, I think we should get a second opinion. Sometimes there are things they can do to help people that have been injured as you have."

"Don't give her false hope." Jathan frowned.

"It wouldn't hurt to try, would it? I think it's the least we should do." She turned back to Sarah Joy. "Perhaps there's nothing they can do. If that's the case, it's okay. You can still do all those things you mentioned, even if you're in a wheelchair. It will be more difficult for you, but you *can* learn to do them. If *you're* willing, Sarah Joy. If there's a will, there's a way."

"Will you help me, Momma?" Her pleading eyes pierced Sarah's.

Sarah looked to Jathan. "I'll help as much as I can."

"How much will that be?" Jathan frowned.

"Well, I don't know. I'll have to talk to..." She looked at Sarah Joy and remembered what Jathan had asked her earlier. "I'll have to see."

Jathan's gaze shot through her. "Where there's a will, there's a way. Isn't that what you said?"

ELEVEN

It was Jathan who would most likely spend the rest of his life caring for Sarah Joy. How was he going to be able to work? What would he do now that their daughter required so much care?

Sarah's spirit warred within her. If only she could stay until Sarah Joy could adjust to her circumstances. Maybe she could bring Claire and Brooke to Pennsylvania.... No, they had to be in school. Not to mention, Mark would never approve. How could she make this work out?

"Sarah, you may go back to Maryland. She will be released this afternoon." Jathan's defeated expression conveyed a sense of disappointment. Or was it sadness?

"What will you do now? Do you have a ride back to your community?" She spoke softly so as not to wake Sarah Joy.

"I will call our driver."

"Let me take you. It's the least I can do," she insisted.

"This is the Sarah I know, always thoughtful." Jathan's mouth curled up at one side ever so slightly. "That is alright. It will probably be easier to say goodbye here."

"Are you certain? I could–"

"Sarah, no. Just go." He briefly touched her hand. "Please. It is too difficult having you here. It gives me hope that maybe we can have more. And the children, they'll expect you to come home."

Sarah nodded. "I understand, Jathan."

Two hours later, Sarah bid goodbye to Jathan and their daughter. She didn't reject Jathan's embrace, although she was certain Mark wouldn't have approved. Her loyalty was with Mark; she knew that. But she couldn't help but feel she should be offering Jathan something more. It was as though she were throwing crumbs to Jathan when he was entitled to a full meal. Of course, she could offer no more.

It was times like this she wished she could talk to someone who'd been through a similar situation. But she was pretty sure she was the only one in the world who was experiencing an ordeal like this. And that realization brought a sense of loneliness.

What she needed to do was pray, she realized. Wasn't it God Who led the way through the darkest valleys? He'd led the children of Israel out of Egypt and through the wilderness. Surely her problem was not too difficult for the God of the Universe to handle. *God, please show me the way. I want to do the right thing. Tell me what to do and I'll do it.*

WAIT.

Had she really heard something or was it just her imagination?

"Wait for what, Lord?" she asked aloud.

She stopped at the traffic light and looked to her right. Hopefully the gentleman in the vehicle next to her didn't think she was crazy. Oh well, let him think whatever he wanted.

As she pulled into her driveway, she glanced at the clock on the dashboard. Almost five. Mark would be arriving home from work in just a little while. Good. She'd have time to prepare a quick something for dinner. Spaghetti sounded good.

A look at the clock on the dining room wall told Sarah that Mark was late. Where was he? Dinner had been ready an hour ago.

Another hour passed. Should she wait for him or go take her shower?

She sighed and headed toward their bedroom.

Even if she didn't take her shower yet, she could get her night clothes ready.

"Sarah?" Mark's voice called from the front door.

"I'm in here," she called.

"Mommy!" Sarah could hear Brooke and Claire's footsteps racing down the hallway.

Sarah bent down and gave both girls a hug and a kiss as soon as they entered her bedroom. "I missed you two."

"Where have you been, Mommy?" Claire asked.

"I was visiting someone in the hospital."

"Who?" Brooke asked.

"Oh. Uh, well...it's someone you don't know."

"You're going to stay with *us* now, right? I don't like you to go." Claire pouted.

"For now." Sarah looked up and saw Mark standing in the doorway.

"For *now*?" His frown told her he wasn't pleased.

"I was going to talk to you about that." She glanced at the girls.

Mark touched the girls' shoulders. "Alright, you two, it's time to say goodnight. Give Mommy a kiss."

Sarah bid Brooke and Claire goodnight. She could hear Mark in the bathroom down the hall as he helped the girls brush their teeth. He was a good daddy. She put dinner away as Mark read the girls a short bedtime story and prayed with them. Sarah briefly wondered what kind of nighttime routine her Amish daughters had.

By the time Mark was finished, she'd returned to the bedroom.

"So, tell me what your plans are, Sarah." She didn't miss Mark's perturbed tone as he closed the door behind himself.

"I don't have plans. I wanted to discuss it with you."

"I'm here. Let's discuss." His abrupt tone was bothersome.

"Can you please not be short tempered with me?"

"How do you expect me to react when my wife's been gone for a whole week? With her *other* husband."

Sarah couldn't hide her frustration. "You know I was at the hospital with Sarah Joy."

"Yeah." He shook his head.

"What's that supposed to mean?"

"I want my wife back, that's what it means. I don't want to hear that you have to go back to Pennsylvania."

"But Sarah Joy needs me."

"*I* need you. *Our* girls need you. Let Jathan figure out what to do with Sarah Joy."

"She's in a wheelchair, Mark! She'll probably never walk again."

Mark frowned. "You know, I'm sorry about that. I really am. But she's not your concern, Sarah. You have a family here."

"She's not my concern? Of course, she's my concern! She's my daughter, Mark. She's named after me." Sarah threw her hands in the air. "How can you even say that?"

"All I know is that before Jathan came along, we had a perfect family—a perfect marriage. Now, we can't even have a conversation without raising our voices. We can't have a conversation where Jathan or your other family doesn't come up. I want *us* back. Is that too much to ask for?"

"You know we can't go back to that life. You know I can't just pretend that my other family doesn't exist."

"I think it's time you made a decision."

"A decision?"

"Yes. Choose which family you want to be a part of."

Sarah shook her head. "I hope you're kidding, Mark. You can't just ask me to give my daughters up."

"Don't you see, Sarah? We can have our family back again. We can have normal. I'm tired of sharing you. Either you leave them or us."

"No."

"Fine. I'll make this easy for you. The girls and I are moving to Maine. You can either go with us or you can stay here. The choice is yours."

Tears burned her eyes. "Choice? What kind of choice is that?"

Mark's arms crossed his chest. He wasn't budging.

"Maine? What's in Maine?"

"My job. I've been offered a promotion."

"So, just like that? You're leaving me?"

"No. I'm the leader, remember? You're supposed to follow."

"Why would you do this to me? You know I can't choose."

"I'm not going to stand by and watch as another man sweeps in and steals my wife's heart. Can't you see it, Sarah? You're already falling in love with Jathan."

"No, I'm not. That's not true."

"It *is* true. Don't deny it. I've seen how your face lights up when you talk about him."

Her face warmed. It was true that she cared for Jathan, but that didn't mean she wanted to leave Mark for him. They had a bond—their children. And she had a maternal responsibility to care for the girls. How could she shirk her duties? Especially now when she was needed most?

"Sarah Joy needs my help, Mark. I'm not going to

leave her. She needs time to adjust to her circumstances and I plan to help her. That's what I wanted to discuss with you."

"You go ahead and do whatever you want, Sarah. It's plain to see which family you value more."

Never in her life had she felt like slapping Mark, but now she came pretty close to it. She took a deep breath and clenched her fists so tightly that her fingernails dug into her skin. "That's ridiculous!"

"No. It's the truth."

"It's impossible to reason with you. I'm going to take my shower now." Sarah turned and began walking down the hall.

"I wasn't done," Mark called after her.

"I am."

"Yeah, that's what I thought."

Sarah closed the bathroom door a little harder than she'd intended to. Hopefully, the girls wouldn't be awakened by her and Mark's conflict. She didn't know if she wanted to cry out of frustration for Mark's lack of sympathy and understanding, or because their marriage was falling apart.

Twenty minutes later, she returned to an empty bedroom. She walked to the living room to find Mark asleep on the sofa. If that was what he wanted, then so be it.

After an hour, she found herself staring at the ceiling in the darkness, waiting for sleep to come. She'd probably break down in tears if she wasn't so upset. *How can he make me choose?* It just wasn't right.

God, I need Your help here. I don't know what I'm supposed to do. Should I do what Pastor Joe recommended and just divorce Jathan? The thought of divorce pained her greatly. She didn't think she could ever bring herself to do it.

It was nearly two in the morning when sleep finally came. Nothing had been resolved. God had once again kept silent.

TWELVE

Sarah awoke to a quiet house. Apparently, Mark had dropped the girls off at school as he'd been doing the past week. What time was it? Glancing at the clock, she realized it was already ten o'clock. *I'd better get moving.*

Today, she was determined to figure some things out. And that meant meeting with Pastor Joe. For better or worse, she needed some answers.

At eleven, she pulled into the church parking lot. Pastor Joe's car was already there. Sarah sighed and walked to the church's administrative office. "Hi, Kristin. Is Pastor Joe in?"

"Do you have an appointment with him today?" The secretary analyzed the planner on her desk.

Sarah frowned. "Uh, no, but I was hoping he'd be free to talk for a few minutes."

"Well, he doesn't have any appointments

scheduled until the afternoon. I'll just go back and ask him if he's available." Kristin's friendly smile always seemed to brighten the room.

"Thanks, Kristin."

Sarah waited, but not for long.

Kristin returned with her usual cheerful demeanor. "He said it's no problem. Go on back."

Sarah nodded her thankfulness and walked through the hallway to the pastor's office.

"Sarah. What can I do for you?" Pastor Joe rose from behind his desk and extended his hand.

She briefly shook it. "I can't bring myself to divorce Jathan, like you suggested."

"I see."

"I mean, how can I justify that according to Scripture? I just don't have peace about it."

Pastor Joe's fingers steepled in front of his chin. "If you don't have peace about it, then I'd advise you not to do it. The last thing a person should do is violate their conscience. I merely suggested it as a solution because I saw no other way."

"Okay. So then, what should I do? Or rather, what would Jesus do?"

"I can't really say what the Lord would do because I have no Scriptural backing. The reason I'd suggested divorce is that you can't be married, even legally speaking, to two people."

"Would you say that by marrying Mark I've committed adultery? I mean, since I was already married to Jathan." This was the first time she'd ever thought of the possibility.

"But you said you'd had amnesia. Did you know you were already married to someone else?"

"No. I had no clue."

"Sarah, God doesn't hold us accountable for what we don't know."

"He doesn't?"

"Here." He handed his Bible to her. "Read this, the highlighted part."

She read the part of the verse he'd underlined. "...for where no law is, there is no transgression."

"That's right. Also, in Romans five, thirteen it says sin is not imputed when there is no law. So, it's just like when a young child dies. He's not held accountable because he wasn't mature enough to discern good and evil. Age of accountability."

"But even though I didn't know it then, I do know it now. How am I supposed to respond?" Sarah frowned. "Since I know now, I'm accountable, right?"

Pastor Joe rubbed his forehead. "I have actually looked into this some, after our previous discussion. According to *the law*, your marriage to Mark would most likely be considered void. When someone marries without all their faculties in place, which is what happened with you because of your amnesia, the courts would issue an annulment. You were married under false pretenses."

Sarah's mouth hung open.

The pastor continued. "However, since the two of you have children together, it makes this matter a little more complicated."

"I just want to know what I'm supposed to do. What's the *right* thing to do?"

"I hate to say it, Sarah, but there is no cut-and-dried answer. This is something *you're* going to have to figure out." Pastor Joe frowned. "Either way, it will be difficult."

"Mark wants to move to Maine with the girls," she said matter-of-factly.

"And you?"

"My Amish daughter, Sarah Joy, was just in a tragic accident. She's in a wheelchair now and she needs help. She's the oldest of Jathan's and my girls so most of the maternal responsibilities have fallen on her shoulders since I've been away. I'm certain she needs her mother. They all do."

"And what about Claire and Brooke?"

"You know I love them dearly. I love all my

children. I wish there were two of me."

"Will you move to Maine with Mark?"

"I can't. How can I when Sarah Joy needs me? I can't just abandon her."

He nodded. "I understand."

"Mark doesn't *have to* move to Maine. He's choosing to." *That* was the thought that bothered her most.

"Just like you're choosing to stay."

"Yeah, I guess I am."

"Do the girls know?"

"No, they don't." Pain ripped through her heart at the thought. How could she tell the girls that she wouldn't be moving with them? "I'm hoping Mark will let them stay here with me."

"So, will you move in with Jathan then?"

Move in with Jathan? The thought had never occurred to her. "No, I hadn't planned on it."

"Do you have the means to live on your own?"

Another thing she hadn't thought of. She hadn't had a job outside the home in years. Not since Brooke was born. "No. Mark makes all the money."

"Where will you live?"

"I haven't thought that far yet."

"You need to consider all these things, Sarah."

"I know." She felt a headache coming on.

"When is Mark moving?"

"I don't know. He just mentioned it last night."

"Well, let me know if there's any way I can be of assistance."

"If you could pray for us that would probably be what we need most. I need wisdom."

"I will continue to pray for your family, Sarah. Would you like me to have Kristin add you to the church's prayer list?"

"As an unspoken request, please. I don't know how Mark would feel if we gave details."

"Alright, then." Pastor Joe nodded. "How about if we pray now, as well?"

"I'd appreciate that." Sarah smiled as the pastor led in prayer.

Mark reached over to turn the heater down and glanced at the manila envelope on the seat next to him. *God, please help me.* He prayed in silence as he traveled home from work. *I don't know what to do here. This Maine thing sounded so far out there at first. I didn't think I'd ever really consider it, but now I'm thinking this could be the answer. Lord, did You bring this along at this time because of what's going on in our lives? Is this opportunity from You?*

You know how much I love Sarah. I don't want to let her go, Lord. I'm ashamed of myself for how short-tempered I've been with her lately, but I'm jealous. I know that's something You understand. I never thought I'd come to a point where I would move away without my wife. It would be really good if she could come with us. But I also realize that she belongs to someone else. God, I can't believe I've been sleeping with another man's wife all these years!

I refuse to blame You for it, although I know that's what the devil wants me to do. I know You can work all these things out for the good and for Your glory. I don't understand it all, but I can't help but think that You brought this situation into our lives for a reason.

He pulled into the driveway and grasped the large envelope from the seat. *Please give me the courage I need, Lord. This isn't going to be easy.*

As Sarah drove back to the house, she was tempted to turn onto the freeway and head toward Lancaster. How was Sarah Joy coping? Jathan had said that ladies from their community would bring meals by to help the family out. That was thoughtful.

How different had life been before she left Jathan? Other than Jathan's drinking, had she been happy? Did they have a good marriage? Did she fit into the Amish community or had they viewed her with caution because she'd previously been an *Englischer*? How would they view her now if she returned? Not that she would.

As soon as she pulled into the driveway, her phone began vibrating.

"Hello?" she answered the call.

"Momma?"

Sarah glanced down at the number. The area code indicated the call was from Lancaster County.

"Sarah Joy? Is this you?"

"I told you he would, Momma! I knew he would," Sarah Joy's voice cried.

"What are you talking about, Sarah Joy?"

"Simon. He...he doesn't want to marry me now." Sarah Joy sniffled. "I told you nobody would want a girl who couldn't walk."

"Shh...it's okay, Sarah Joy." She attempted to reassure her daughter.

"No, it's not. It's not okay at all."

"Remember what *Dat* said? A good man will overlook your limitations. Someone worth marrying will love you for who you are, not for what you can do." Jathan had been wise to utter those words.

"My heart hurts real bad, Momma."

Sarah could hear the tears through the phone and

she longed to offer her daughter a hug. "I know it does. I'm sorry, baby."

"When are you coming back home?"

It was a simple question but, of course, Sarah couldn't give any concrete answers at present. "I don't know, honey. I may come visit this weekend."

"Why? Why can't you stay, Momma?"

Telling her daughter the truth would only cause more pain and make Jathan upset with her. "I just can't, Sarah Joy."

"You love someone else, don't you? I saw you with that man. You left *Dat* for him, didn't you?" She spat the words out like spoiled soup.

"Sarah Joy..."

"It's true, isn't it, Momma? You left us for *him*."

"No, it's not like that, honey."

"Who is he, then? Your brother?"

"No." Sarah sighed. "Remember your father said that I'd been in an accident?"

"*Jah.*"

Mark pulled into the driveway next to her car. "Look, Sarah Joy. I need to go now."

"Don't go, Momma! Please, don't hang up. I...I miss talking to you."

"I know you do, honey. We can talk when I come on Sunday, okay?"

"Will you come to meeting with us?"

"No, but I should be there afterwards. I'll talk to you then. I love you, Sarah Joy. Goodbye."

"Bye, Momma."

"Who was that?"

Sarah put her phone back into her purse. "It was Sarah Joy."

"Figures."

Sarah bit her tongue. She wouldn't voice her thoughts, as they would only lead to more strife.

Mark handed her an envelope as they walked into the house.

"What's this?" Sarah frowned.

"Open it. You'll see."

THIRTEEN

Sarah pulled out a small stack of papers stapled together.

"I took the liberty of visiting a lawyer today. He said we didn't need a divorce. Those are annulment papers. Since you're already married to Jathan, our marriage is technically invalid. This just takes it a step further."

Sarah's jaw dropped. "You want a divorce?"

"I told you, it's not a divorce. It's an annulment. Since you weren't fully aware, mentally speaking, because of your amnesia when you married me, we're entitled to an annulment. Neither one of us had any business getting married to each other."

"And you're fine with this? That's it? You're just going to pack up and leave like we never existed?"

"Don't go crying on me, Sarah. We're adults. We need to treat this like we are. I don't blame you, because it's really not your fault. I'm sure that if you'd known you were married, you never would have agreed to marry me, right?"

She frowned but agreed.

"And if I'd known *you* were married, I wouldn't have thought twice about it. Come here." He pulled her into an embrace. "We had a lot of good years together, right? We have some cute kids. Not a total loss, wouldn't you say?"

"What about the girls?"

"We'll have joint custody. I'll have them for six months with me in Maine. You'll have them for six months in Pennsylvania."

"Pennsylvania?"

"Do you not intend to go back to your husband?"

"Mark! Listen to yourself. Why are you acting so nonchalant about all this? Don't you even care?"

"Sarah, this isn't easy for me. I'm acting a lot tougher than I feel, believe me. But I realize this is what has to happen if we want our lives to move forward. We've got to make the best of it." He rubbed her shoulders. "I've loved you with everything I have, Sarah. And don't think this isn't killing me, because it is. But, as they say, all good things must come to an end."

"I don't want you to leave. I love you." She brushed a tear away.

"I know. That's exactly why I have to. Sarah, you're married to another man. I can't share you any more than he can."

"When are you leaving?"

"Saturday."

"*This* Saturday?"

"Yes. The sooner we're separated, the better."

"I don't know if I can do this. Jathan is virtually a stranger to me."

"He's your husband. There's got to be a reason you married him in the first place, right?"

She nodded.

"You'll find that reason again."

"I wish things could be different."

"Me, too. But this is our reality." He lifted her chin. "Let's not hold a grudge, okay?"

She nodded. "You seem to have it all figured out."

"No. I have nothing figured out. And when I do think I have it figured out, it will change. That's life—always changing. The way I see it is we can take this lot we've been given and become bitter over it, or we can let it transform us into something better."

"I'll try my best."

"I know that I'm a better person for knowing you. You've taught me a lot about life and love. I'll never forget that." He gently kissed her forehead. "Thank you for loving me, Sarah."

She felt like she loved him even more now than ever. How in the world could she let him go? "I don't want to lose you, Mark." Tears blurred her vision once again.

"That's enough. Let's not make this any harder than it already is." He took a step back and shoved his hands into his pockets. Was he emotionally distancing himself?

"How are we going to tell the girls?"

"I think it'll be best if you let me handle it. I'm not sure how much they'll even understand. Just tell them goodbye, and I'll explain things better to them when we get to Maine. I won't speak negatively of you, I promise." His gaze sobered. "And I hope you'll give me the same courtesy."

"Will they be able to call me?"

"As much as your Amish community will allow, I guess." He shrugged.

"I don't think that will be a problem. Maybe we can even do a video call once in a while."

Mark smiled. "I'm sure the girls would love that, if you can swing it."

"What about the house?"

"I plan to talk to a realtor tomorrow. If you decide you'd like to stay here for a while, I'll wait on selling. I'm sure you'll want time to discuss things with Jathan."

Sarah took a deep breath and nodded. "You're sure you want to do this?"

"Sarah, please stop asking me that. No, I don't *want* to do this. To tell the truth, I wish that Jathan and your past didn't exist. But they do. And *because* they do, it has to be this way. I know it's hard. Unbearably so. But we must continue to move forward. God has something planned. We just need to trust Him through this."

Where was Mark finding this strength? She wished she could have just an ounce of it. "I know. This is all so sudden."

"In a year from now, we'll have a new normal."

"It's hard to think of a year from now. So much can happen in a year."

"We mustn't fear the future, Sarah. If God placed us on this path, He will surely lead us out."

When had Mark's faith ever been so strong? Perhaps this ordeal had strengthened his walk with God. For that, Sarah was truly thankful. "Mark, what if Jathan isn't even saved?"

"You haven't discussed salvation with him?"

Sarah frowned. "No."

Mark rubbed the stubble on his chin. "That sounds like an opportunity."

"I'm scared."

"Of what?"

"I'm an outsider moving into an Amish community. What if they don't want me there? What if I can't make it work? What if—"

"Sarah. You will just have to trust God."

Of course, that was all she *could* do. Her whole world was about to turn upside down.

FOURTEEN

$\mathcal{E}$xplaining to the girls that Daddy was going to Maine without Mommy had been an emotionally demanding task. Sarah was certain the girls didn't truly understand the implications of their circumstances. They probably thought it was to be an extended vacation. When they did eventually discover the truth of their new reality, they'd be devastated. But Sarah didn't want to think about that right now.

She'd held her tears back until Mark's vehicle drove away, hauling the precious cargo they'd created together. She thought the dull ache in her heart might consume her. Not only would she not see the girls for at least six months, but she'd never be held in Mark's strong arms again. If someone would have told her a year ago that this would be her future, she never would have believed it.

She had yet to tell Jathan of Mark's sudden departure. That could wait till tomorrow. Sarah briefly deliberated whether she would attend meeting with Jathan and their girls in Amish country or if she'd go to Pastor Joe's service. She finally decided on the latter, since this could possibly be her final visit to her home church of the past five years.

Now, Sarah walked through the silent house that she and Mark had once shared with their girls. Oh, how she'd miss them all. She'd spent hours in tears last night and now the lack of sleep was beginning to take a toll on her. But she wouldn't take a nap for fear of arriving late in Lancaster. She had a promise to keep.

Two hours later, she drove up the lane to Jathan's farm. Wouldn't he be surprised when he learned the current state of events? Sarah's thoughts on the matter were bittersweet. She knew that her place was to be with Jathan now, but how could she just move forward? How could she forget about Mark and the girls and the last ten years of her life? Why had God brought her down this tumultuous path?

Jathan came to her vehicle's door the moment it rolled to a stop. Clearly, he was eager to see her.

Her opened door was met with a frown from Jathan, a stark contrast from the excitement he'd exhibited just seconds ago. "Sarah, what is wrong?

You look like you've been crying."

Sarah looked to the house where a couple of their daughters stood near the door. "May you and I talk alone?"

"*Jah*, of course." He looked back to the house and realized the source of her reticence. "I will tell the girls to wait for lunch. Let's go for a walk."

Sarah nodded and watched as Jathan informed the girls of their plans. The girls promptly returned inside the house, and Sarah met Jathan at the porch.

"Come." He nodded toward the pasture and she walked in step by his side. When they were far enough away from the house, Jathan spoke. "What is wrong, Sarah?"

She took a deep breath and tried to keep her tears at bay. "Mark and the girls are gone."

"What do you mean by 'gone'?" He frowned.

"Mark left yesterday. He moved to Maine. The girls are staying with him."

Jathan stared at her in silence for what seemed like an eternity. "I don't understand, Sarah."

"Mark and I are getting an annulment." Sarah studied Jathan's puzzled face. "Do you know what that means?"

"No."

"Well, it's basically a releasing of our marriage vows."

"A divorce?"

"No, this is different. But at the same time, it's similar. You see, because I had amnesia when Mark and I married, I didn't fully comprehend what I was doing. I was mentally incompetent. If I'd known that I was already married, I wouldn't have married Mark. Legally speaking, Mark and I cannot even be married because I'm married to you."

"I see."

"You do?"

"This means that you and Mark aren't married anymore. And that you are still married to me." She attempted to decipher his expression.

"Basically. But I don't know how that all works as far as the paperwork goes."

"Paperwork?"

"For the annulment."

"I see. Does this mean you will move back to Lancaster?" The hopefulness in his tone couldn't be masked.

She shrugged. "I don't know. That's kind of what I wanted to discuss with you. What do *you* want?"

Jathan swallowed and his eyes seemed to mist briefly. "Sarah, you know I love you. I always have."

Sarah nodded.

"I want you to be happy." He looked away. Was he

afraid of his next words? "Do...do you think you could be happy with me again?"

"Firstly, I want to do what's right before God. But, to answer your question, I'm willing to give it a try."

"You..." He swallowed. "You will move in with me and live here?"

Sarah didn't miss the sparkle in his eye. Her heartbeat quickened. She nodded. "If that's what you want."

"I have prayed for this day for many years." This time, tears did indeed spring to his eyes. "*Der Herr* be praised!"

"It might not be easy for us, Jathan. I've changed a lot since you last knew me. I don't know how it will be for us." She didn't want to get his hopes up only to crush his spirit again. What if things didn't go well?

"I will win your love again, Sarah." His expression exuded confidence.

"We will need to tell the girls about my marriage to Mark. We'll have Brooke and Claire living with us for half of the year."

Jathan frowned.

"You don't approve?"

"It is okay. We will tell the girls about your accident and explain it all to them. And they will be happy for two more sisters."

"I'm a little concerned about your Amish church. Will your friends look down on you? On us?"

"It does not matter what they say. This is *our* family." He took her hand. "When we married before, there were some that spoke against us. After you learned our language and were baptized into the church, the busybodies quieted down. It will take some time for them to get used to it, but it will be okay."

"You're sure?"

Jathan nodded with a reassuring smile.

"Did I have friends in the community before I left?"

"Some. My sister Ruth came over to visit quite a bit."

Sarah smiled. "I thought there was something special about her."

FIFTEEN

This could not be happening. *Sarah has come back home to stay?* Jathan's heart nearly exploded with emotion. He had to get away to gather himself together, lest he break down in front of Sarah and the girls. What would Sarah think if she saw him in all his weakness?

"I need to go out," he told Sarah.

"But we haven't even eaten lunch yet."

"Eat without me. I must go. I'll be back." He quickly dismissed himself and rushed out the door.

Jathan could hear the chairs scraping the wooden floor as the girls no doubt took their places at the table. The sounds became more and more inaudible the further away from the house his feet traveled.

Once in the midst of the cornfield, Jathan fell to his knees. He couldn't help the rush of tears. "*Gott* in Heaven above, You have been so *gut* to me! I don't deserve all Your blessings. *Denki* for my beloved Sarah. Thank You for bringing her back to me and giving me a second chance. Please help us, *Vatter*. Help Sarah to love me once again. Make her a *gut mudder* for our *kinner*. Help me to love Sarah as I should—as she deserves to be loved. Please heal our hearts and bind us together." No matter if the neighbors heard his soulful outburst, although it was unlikely being a half-mile away.

For several minutes afterward, he knelt there in the cold soil with his head down in silent prayer. He arose from the dirt and turned around to find Sarah standing near. He quickly swiped at the tears and frowned.

"That was beautiful, Jathan." Sarah's eyes misted.

He swallowed and took a step closer. "It was?"

"I don't know if I've ever seen a man cry over me. Or pray like that."

"Like what?"

"With all your heart." She came close enough that Jathan inhaled the scent of her lovely perfume. "That...it was amazing."

When Sarah's lips met his, he didn't dare ask any questions. No, he simply pulled her close and indulged in the moment. Her soft lips and warm hands around his neck brought back vivid memories of years past. This was his wife! The one who had been lost for the last ten years of his life. And now God wrought a miracle in their lives. Sarah was back in his arms again.

Jathan didn't know how long they'd been out there for, but he was certain their lunch was cold by now. As they walked back to the house hand in hand, the look of pleasure on their girls' faces wasn't to be missed. He read them loud and clear, *we are glad Momma is home again.*

Since hearing Jathan's emotional prayer in the cornfield and seeing his tear-stained shirt, Sarah had found him irresistible. Had God already begun to knit their hearts together?

She had no intention of moving into Jathan's bedroom the first week she returned, but that was exactly what happened. It was as though a magnet had pulled her into his arms and she felt helpless to resist. She didn't *want* to resist. No, this was exactly where she belonged – in Jathan's strong embrace.

This was her husband. This felt right and good. The last ten years of separation seemed to disappear in mere minutes.

And the memories—they began rushing back.

Sarah laughed out loud. "I know you. I *know* you, Jathan!"

He kissed her forehead and smiled. "What do you mean?"

"This room. This furniture. You. It's all familiar to me." She untangled a strand of hair with her hand and looked around. "Did I...were our children born here in this room?"

His jaw dropped. "*Jah*. You remember?"

She closed her eyes and attempted to process this new information, which really wasn't new at all. "There was an older woman."

"That was Susan, the midwife." Jathan nodded.

"And it seemed like the baby took a long time." Sarah frowned. "Did I lose it?"

Jathan remained silent, his gaze sober.

"Jathan." She cradled his face in her hands. "Did we lose a baby?" Sorrow suddenly filled her heart.

"Our boy." Moisture in Jathan's eyes tainted his previous joy.

"We had a boy?"

"*Der Herr* took him home." Jathan frowned. "Then He took you away."

"I left you after our baby died?"

He nodded briefly.

She hated to think she'd leave Jathan during a time

of immense grief. "Why would I do that?"

"It was my fault our *boppli* died."

"What do you mean, Jathan?"

"I'd been drinking. You needed the midwife to come but I was too *dumm* to fetch her. The girls went to the phone shanty but by the time Susan finally arrived, the *boppli* was gone. He got stuck. I couldn't help you."

Regret blanketed Jathan's face.

"I'm sure it wasn't your fault, Jathan." She gently touched his forearm.

"It was. Susan told me so."

She shook her head. "We all make mistakes."

"Not like that. Not something that causes another person's death. That's unforgivable."

"No, Jathan. That's not true. God will forgive anything if we come to Him and repent."

"You needed me, Sarah! You needed me and I failed you. How can you forgive me for that?"

"Jathan, I'm not perfect either. We all do things worthy of condemnation. Without Jesus shedding His blood on the cross, I would still be in my sins and on my way to Hell." She lifted his chin. "But I asked God for His forgiveness. I asked Him to save me and He did."

"How do you know?"

"Because God said so. *He that hideth his sins shall not prosper. But whoso confesseth and forsaketh them shall find mercy.* The Bible says, *for whosoever shall call upon the name of the Lord shall be saved.* That's God's promise to us."

"I haven't been a *gut* man."

"None of us are good in God's sight. Even the best of us are sinners. That's *why* we need Jesus. Only He can make us righteous." Sarah studied her husband. "Jathan, have you ever asked Jesus to save you?"

"*Nee.* Bishop Wagler and the leaders don't approve of this teaching."

"But this is what God's Word teaches. Do they not teach the Bible?"

"Some. But we must abide by the *Ordnung*—the ordinances of our church."

"Ordinances?"

"*Jah.* Our rules."

"I'd like to show you something, Jathan." Sarah smiled.

SIXTEEN

Jathan stared at Sarah, his conscience wary. Her leaving had obviously opened her up to new teachings—dangerous teachings he'd been warned about his entire life.

He watched as she retrieved her Bible from the dresser drawer. When she opened it up, he noticed many markings inside. Forbidden markings. Only the leaders in his Amish community had been allowed to write in their Bibles—had been gifted to study and understand the true meaning of the passages therein.

"Tell me what this means to you, Jathan." Sarah opened the book to a certain passage.

He examined the words. *And you, being dead in your sins and the uncircumcision of your flesh, hath he quickened together with him, having forgiven you all trespasses; Blotting out the handwriting of ordinances that was against us, which was contrary to us, and took it out of the way, nailing it to his cross.* "I don't understand this," he admitted.

"The Apostle Paul is writing to the church in Colossi. He's explaining that now that they have trusted in Christ, they are no longer dead in their sins but are now alive in Christ and have been forgiven. When Jesus died on the cross, the laws also known as the *ordinances*, were nailed to the cross and blotted out. Meaning that all righteous demands of the law were fulfilled in Jesus. We just need to trust in what He did."

He read through the passage once again and pondered the words.

"Here is another place the Bible speaks of ordinances. Ephesians chapter two."

Jathan read the whole chapter and marveled at the words. "This is not what our leaders teach."

"Why not?" Sarah frowned.

"I do not know. I've always been told that when someone claims they are saved, they are full of worldly pride. But that is not what this says." He looked back at the passage and read the words again, this time aloud. "*For by grace are ye saved through faith; and that not of yourselves: it is a gift of God: Not of works, lest any man should boast.* And verse fifteen says the same thing about the ordinances that those other verses said."

"That's right. When I claim that I'm saved, it's not because of anything that *I* have done. I've only accepted God's gift of grace that is available to everyone. Jesus is the one who paid the price for my salvation. If I'm proud of something, I'm proud to belong to Him and of what He's done."

"How have we been wrong all this time? Why would they not teach us what the Bible says?"

"I don't know. Maybe they've never truly studied it for themselves." Sarah shrugged. "Do you want to show them what it says?"

Jathan shook his head. "No. I cannot do that, Sarah. They will accuse me of being prideful and acting like I know it all."

"No one knows it all, but there are some people that may know more than others. Do they not believe they can learn from anyone else?"

Jathan grimaced. "Sarah, our teachings have been passed down from our ancestors for hundreds of years. They're pretty set in their ways. They will not listen." *Especially to a woman*, he'd wanted to say but didn't.

"So, instead of studying a claim made by someone, they just dismiss it? Are they afraid they might have to admit that they could be wrong?"

He heard the indignation in her voice.

"I don't know."

"So, because of someone's *pride*, others end up dying in their sins and going to Hell?" She was pacing the room now. "We have to speak up, Jathan."

"I told you they will not listen. They will put us under the *Bann*." Of course, Sarah was already under the *Bann*, unbeknownst to her. Jathan would tell her when the time was right.

"Which means?"

"We will not be able to fellowship with others in the community."

"You've got to be kidding."

Jathan shook his head.

"And if we do?"

Jathan admitted that he loved Sarah's persistence. She seemed determined. "All our friends and family will be warned not to talk to us or have anything to do with us. If they do, they will be put in the *Bann* too."

"Do you have any idea how oppressive and controlling that sounds? Jathan, how can you live in a community like this?"

He shrugged. "This is all I've ever known, Sarah. My family is here. This is my life."

"But Jesus wants us to have abundant life. You can't have abundant life if you're forced to live according to something you don't believe in."

"I cannot leave, Sarah. My folks, my siblings, my farm, my *kinner*, my whole life is here."

"But, is *God* here?"

"*Der Herr* is everywhere."

"That's true. But if He's not in the hearts of the people in the church, of what value is it?"

He had to put his foot down. "We cannot go to the leaders, Sarah."

"What about the people? What if we share those Bible passages with them privately?"

Jathan's brow rose. "I don't know. But some will surely tell the leaders what we are doing."

"Don't you think we should at least try? They need to hear the Truth, Jathan. They have a right to know that living by the church ordinances isn't going to earn them a place in Heaven."

Jathan moved close to Sarah and gently caressed her cheek. "Have I ever told you how much I love you?"

She smiled, then gave him a look. "You're changing the subject."

"No, not really." He rubbed her upper arm. "We can try to talk to the family, but I do not know where it will end up."

"That's all I'm asking for, Jathan. We'll tell them and leave the results up to God." She nodded and studied him. "But what about you? Have *you* ever asked Jesus to save you?"

"Can't say that I have. But I reckon now is as good a time as any."

This brought another beautiful smile from Sarah.

"What do I do? Is there a special thing to say?"

She laughed. "No, honey. You just pour your heart out to God and ask Him to save you."

SEVENTEEN

S arah's heart soared with joy. To be able to share the Gospel with her husband, and for him to accept Jesus as his Saviour, had truly been a blessing. But there was still an entire community steeped in darkness. They needed to hear the Good News as well. Jathan's whole family, his friends, his neighbors, and, of course, their girls, needed Jesus. What a privilege she had to be the one to share God's love with them!

Perhaps *this* had been the reason God allowed all these events in her life. Things were finally beginning to make sense. She felt like calling Mark and sharing the news of Jathan's salvation with him. But she wouldn't. The less she thought about Mark, the better it was for her and Jathan's relationship. She quickly dismissed the sharp pain that threatened to dampen her spirit.

"Jathan, do you think this might be the reason God let these things happen?"

"What do you mean? I lost you for ten years of our lives. How can that be God's doing?"

"Well, think about it. If I hadn't left, I wouldn't have met Mark. It was Mark who took me to his church. That's where I heard the Gospel and became a Christian. My parents went to church after I invited them, and they found Jesus too. Now, *you're* saved and who knows how many other people will find the Lord because of it."

Jathan frowned, still unconvinced.

"Just think about it, Jathan. God allowed me to go away for a *season* so we could have *eternity* together."

He stroked his beard. "Perhaps."

"There's a greater plan at work here. God wants *all* people to be saved. Jesus died for the whole world, not just a chosen few. He loves each person dearly and desires to spend eternity with them. Just as you longed for me while I was gone, God longs to bring peace and joy to the hearts of men and women everywhere. Isn't it amazing that *we* get to be a part of that? Isn't it wonderful that you have the *privilege* of sharing God's love with those you love the most?" Sarah couldn't remember a time she'd been this jazzed about her faith.

"I just don't know if I have the right words to say to my family. They don't regard my opinions very highly because of my drinking, which resulted in your leaving. They don't think I can manage my family well. They will be wary of you because you've been *Englisch*. I'm not sure they'll listen to either of us."

"We can't let fear stop us, Jathan. If there's anything God has taught me in this life, it's that. All we can do is tell them. It is the Holy Spirit that will draw their hearts to Him. Remember, God created them and He loves them more than we do."

Jathan smiled. "You are very wise, Sarah. I'm glad God made you my wife."

Sarah laughed. "I don't know about that—the wise part, I mean."

Jathan moved closer. "What about the other part?"

"I think I'm content with being your wife."

His brow rose. "You *think*?"

"Well, we haven't been together all that long so I really don't have much to go on." That didn't sound too great, did it? "I mean, I'm happy with what I've experienced so far."

Jathan gently touched her face and smiled. "What can I do to make you certain?" He bent down and pressed his lips to her neck just behind her ear.

Sarah giggled at the tickling sensation his facial hair

elicited. "That's a good start," she murmured.

"Oh, yeah?"

Jathan continued his romantic notions and, with each advance, the temperature rose another degree.

His exhilarating kiss found hers as though a caged animal had been unleashed, and she couldn't help but acquiesce.

Sarah trembled under her husband's caress "Jathan..." she whispered breathlessly. Her heart fluttered with emotions too complicated to explain.

"Come, my love." Jathan whisked her off her feet as though she weighed no more than a flake of alfalfa hay.

$\sim$

Sarah sat next to Jathan and studied their intertwined fingers. She heard his voice as he spoke to the children, but she was reliving moments of passion they'd experienced the evening before. Jathan had been different than what she'd expected—he'd been so loving and gentle. Had that been one of the things that caused her to fall in love with him in the first place? His kindheartedness was like none she'd ever known. His genuine care struck her as remarkable.

"What's that smile for?" Jathan squeezed her hand.

She bit her bottom lip, not wanting to share

anything intimate in the presence of the girls.

"Well?"

Sarah smiled and shook her head.

Mirth sparkled in his eyes and he leaned close. "You can tell me."

She glanced at the girls then inclined toward Jathan's ear. "I was thinking about last night," she whispered.

His brow shot up. "Oh?"

She nodded and delighted in the hint of color that splashed across Jathan's features.

Jathan cleared his throat and he turned back to the girls. "Like I was saying, your *mamm* and I wanted to read some Scriptures with you this evening."

"I'd like that," their youngest daughter, Julie, said, moving to sit next to her mother on the couch.

Sarah smiled and draped her arm around Julie.

"I wanted to sit by Momma," Becky protested.

Jathan released Sarah's hand. "I can share her." He winked and moved to one of the hickory rockers.

Warmth filled Sarah's heart as she observed Jathan's selflessness. He'd do anything for his girls. What love!

Sarah's eyes darted to Sarah Joy, who was still adjusting to her wheelchair. Jathan had already built a ramp to accommodate maneuvering up and down the front porch, and he'd also moved her bedroom downstairs. They hadn't had their talk yet, but Sarah Joy said she didn't mind waiting a couple of days since she knew now that Momma would be staying. Sarah determined to talk to her daughter tomorrow.

After Jathan and Sarah shared the passages from the Bible and discussed them with the girls, Sarah asked them if they'd like to be saved. This brought a few more questions from the girls, and after they understood, every one of the girls said they wanted to trust Jesus as their Saviour. They couldn't get over the fact that God made the way to Heaven so simple.

No doubt, they would have questions at times and the enemy would cause them to doubt their faith. Sarah was sure to show them God's promises—promises they could stand on and cling to no matter what came their way.

"Thank you for coming back, Momma. We love you." Those were the words Mary spoke before retiring for the evening, and the other girls and Jathan echoed her sentiments. Sarah hadn't felt this fulfilled for as long as she could remember. Falling asleep in Jathan's arms was another blessing for which she felt unworthy.

God had been so good.

EIGHTEEN

"**M**omma, can we talk now?"

Sarah turned from the sink at Sarah Joy's voice. "Sure, let me just dry my hands and call Mary and Anna in to finish up the dishes."

She promptly called her other two daughters, and they entered the kitchen with smiles. She was thankful for the girls' enthusiasm. She knew it stemmed from the fact that she was back home with them and they desired to please her.

"Thank you, girls. Maybe we can make a special treat later." This brought even more excitement from the girls and they chatted among themselves in Pennsylvania Dutch while working together. If only things could always be this joyful.

Sarah turned back to Sarah Joy, who tried her best to be cheerful. Perhaps times weren't happy for everyone in the family.

"Would you like to go outside, Sarah Joy?"

"*Jah.*"

"Do you need help getting outside?"

"Just with the door, if you would. I can do it myself, but it's a lot easier if someone helps."

Sarah moved to hold the door open while her daughter wheeled herself outside. "We can just sit out on the porch."

"I'd like that, Momma."

Sarah let her daughter find her preferred spot on the porch, and then she sat down on the rocker next to her.

They sat quietly for a few moments and enjoyed the peacefulness of nature. The cool breeze persuaded a strand of hair under Sarah Joy's *kapp* to break loose. "I can't believe it's this close to Christmas and we've had so little snow."

Sarah smiled. "I'm sure January and February will make up for December's lack of snowfall."

"*Jah.*" Sarah Joy nodded. "Momma, will you tell me who that man is? The one you came here with before."

"I think your father wanted to be here when we discussed that. Maybe we can talk about that tonight, if your father doesn't mind."

"Okay."

"Would you like to discuss what you mentioned on the phone?"

"You mean about Simon?"

"Is that your boyfriend?"

"He was..." Sarah Joy's voice trailed off.

Sarah waited for her daughter to continue.

Sarah Joy sniffled and swiped at a tear. "I'm sorry, Momma. It's just, I loved Simon. I thought we would get married someday. But now, he doesn't even want to see me."

"Sarah Joy, if Simon doesn't love you for you then he doesn't deserve you. You don't want to be married to someone like that. You want someone who will stay by your side no matter what happens, someone who will love through the good *and* bad times."

"But you left *Dat* and us."

"Yeah, I guess I did. I think your father and I were going through a lot at that time. Sometimes, even if you love someone, you need to get away from everything to recharge your batteries."

"Batteries?"

"What I mean is, sometimes our soul needs refreshment. Do you understand what I mean?"

"I think I might."

"Well, I can't say for sure, but I think that's what

141

happened with your father and me. We were both struggling and neither one of us knew how to deal with it. We should have turned to God in our time of need, but we didn't know God very well at the time."

"But you know Him now."

"That's right. And that's why I think there's nothing your father and I can't get through if we keep God at the center of our lives."

"I'm glad. I like having you here again, Momma."

"And I like being here." Sarah smiled and grasped her daughter's hand. "Sarah Joy, have you ever considered that Simon might not be the one God has chosen for you?"

"But I want him to be the one. My heart hurts when he's not here."

"I think your emotions might be getting in the way of your judgment."

"What do you mean?"

"Sometimes our heart deceives us into thinking something is good for us when it is not. This can lead to even greater heartbreak in the future. We can't see what's up ahead, but God can. If Simon's not the one for you, you can trust that God has a better plan. One thing I've learned is that God can always be trusted. He always knows what's best, and He's wiser than we can ever comprehend."

"It's hard, Momma."

"I know it is, honey. God can give you the strength you need. His strength is made perfect in weakness. Sarah Joy, you can go to God with anything, anytime."

"Sometimes I feel like He doesn't care."

"Those are your emotions deceiving you again. The devil wants you to think that God doesn't care, because he wants you to live a defeated life. God tells us to cast our cares on Him because He cares for us. Sarah Joy, God loves you more than anyone ever will. He created you. You are precious to Him."

"Momma..." Sarah Joy suddenly stopped.

Sarah waited a few moments, but her daughter kept silent. "What is it, Sarah Joy?" she prodded.

A look of sheer amazement filled her features. "You've been with God, haven't you?"

Sarah's heart leapt. "What do you mean?"

"I don't know how for sure, but I can tell that you've been with Jesus. You seem so close to Him, like you know Him and He talks to you."

Sarah smiled. "I'm glad that you can see that. You're right."

"I want to know Him too."

"You can, honey. When you asked Jesus into your life last night, that was the first step. If you want to know Him better, you need to spend some time reading His Word. The Bible will be a lamp to your feet and a light to your path, showing you where to walk."

Sarah Joy reached for her mother, and Sarah moved close so she could wrap her arms around her. "Thank you, Momma. Please, don't ever leave us again."

"I don't plan to."

NINETEEN

Jathan eyed his five beautiful daughters and his gorgeous wife. How did he ever fall this far into God's good graces? It was surely nothing *he'd* ever done. He was a sinner and he knew it. These blessings were clearly only by the grace of God.

"I think we should pray before we begin our discussion," Sarah suggested.

"Good idea." Jathan smiled and bowed his head in silent prayer. He then looked up at each of the girls. "Your momma and I have some important things to talk about with you, but I want to know if any of you have questions of your own that you'd like answered."

The girls looked at each other, and Jathan wondered if they were too timid to speak.

Sarah Joy raised her hand. "Who was the man that came with Momma?"

Jathan looked to Sarah. "Before we answer *that* question, I think we need to start at the beginning."

Sarah Joy nodded. "Okay."

He continued. "Your father used to have a problem with drinking, and because of it and other circumstances, your mother left. That was about ten years ago, so some of you may not remember."

"I don't remember," Julie said.

Jathan nodded. "You weren't yet two, Julie."

"I remember Momma a little bit," Becky added.

Jathan nodded and continued. "When Momma was gone, she had a really bad car accident. I didn't know anything about it. The accident caused your momma to forget everything and everyone, so she didn't remember that she was Amish and lived with us. So, Momma went back to her folks' place and lived there with them.

"Since Momma didn't know she was married and had a family already, she met another man and married him. Sarah Joy, *that* was the man that was here with Momma. His name is Mark. Your momma and Mark had two *bopplin* together, both *maed*. They are five and seven years old."

"Would they be our sisters, then?" Anna asked with a slight bounce.

Sarah spoke now. "They're your half-sisters."

The girls looked at each other and smiled.

Mary frowned. "But Momma's married to someone else?"

"Was," Jathan corrected. "God brought your momma back to us." He reached for Sarah's hand, and their fingers intertwined.

"Where are the girls?" Sarah Joy asked. "Will they be here for Christmas?"

Sarah answered, "No. They're in Maine with their father. They will come to live with us during the summer. But you'll be able to meet them over the phone before then."

"Where's Maine?" Anna asked.

"It's up north. It borders Canada and the Atlantic Ocean," Sarah said.

"Have *you* ever been to the ocean, Momma?" Julie's eyes grew wide.

"Yes, honey. Have you?"

"Nope. That's a long way for a horse to walk," Julie said.

"Yeah, you're right." Sarah laughed, then smiled at Jathan. "Have *you* ever been to the ocean?"

Jathan shook his head. "Can't say I have. Maybe we can take a vacation there one of these days."

The girls squealed with delight.

"Everybody should see the ocean at least once,"

Sarah insisted. "It's amazing."

"I've heard." Jathan squeezed Sarah's hand.

Julie raised her hand. "I have a question."

"What is it, honey?" Sarah asked.

"Are you and *Dat* gonna have more *bopplin*?" she blurted out.

"Julie, *nee*!" Becky warned.

"That's okay," Sarah assured. She looked to Jathan and smiled. "If God is willing."

Jathan's heart soared at the thought of having more *bopplin* around the house. Was God giving them a second chance at *everything*? It sure seemed that way.

⁓

"Momma, can I ask you a question?" Sarah Joy turned to Sarah after the others had gone to their upstairs rooms for the evening.

"Sarah Joy, please say *may I ask you a question* not *can*. Do you know the difference between the two words?" Sarah corrected.

Sarah Joy shook her head.

"Well, when you ask if you *can* do something, you're asking if you are physically able to do it. For example, you ask 'Can I lift up a car?' to which I would say, 'No, you can't. It's too heavy for you.' So, *can* is the wrong word to use if you are asking permission. If

148

you want permission for something, use the word *may*. As in, 'Momma, may I ask you a question?' to which I would say, 'Yes, you may ask me a question.' Understand?"

"Yes, I understand now. Thank you for teaching me, Momma." Sarah Joy smiled. "*May* I ask you a question now?"

Sarah smiled. "Yes, you may."

"Okay. I didn't want to ask this question with *Dat* here because I don't want to hurt him."

Sarah frowned, then nodded for Sarah Joy to continue.

"Do you still love Mark?"

Now this was a question she hadn't been expecting. But it was an honest one that required an honest answer. "Well, Sarah Joy, I've always had a philosophy on that. I believe true love is eternal. I don't think you can love someone with all your heart and then just stop loving them. Your love for them will always be. It may be buried deep within your heart never to see the light of day again, but it's still there."

Sarah Joy frowned. "That's how I feel about Simon. Like I'll always love him."

"Sarah Joy, it's so important that you're careful who you give your heart to. Your love is a precious gift, one that's meant for the person God wants you to spend your life with. Do not give it away freely. The Bible tells us to guard our heart, because out of it are the issues of life. It is hard for the rest of our being not to be affected when our heart is vulnerable."

"But what if I can't find the right person?"

"You don't need to look for the right person. Just follow God and do what's right, and when it is God's perfect timing, *He* will bring that person along. Sarah Joy, you're young. You don't need to be in a hurry. Just pray and trust in God's will for your life."

A knock drew Sarah's attention to the door.

Sarah Joy drew in a quick breath. "*Ach*, it's Simon," she whispered.

She could tell by his knock? "Do you want to talk to him?"

"*Jah*, it's fine."

Sarah moved to open the door and discovered her daughter was correct. "Simon?"

A clean fresh smell emanated from Sarah Joy's former beau, along with the faint scent of cologne.

"*Jah*. Is Sarah Joy home?" He removed his hat from his damp hair and turned it several times with his hands.

A gust of cool air blew in from outside. "Yes, Sarah Joy's here. Would you like to come in?"

"Uh, *jah*, *denki*."

Although she was still learning about the Amish way of doing things, Jathan had already clued her in on how courtship worked within their community. She realized that Simon could be there for several hours, depending on the reason for his visit. By all appearances, Sarah guessed this was to be a positive social call.

"Sarah Joy, do you need anything before I retire for the evening?"

"*Nee*, Momma. I'll be fine." Sarah Joy's eyes sparkled.

"Okay." Sarah embraced her daughter. "Goodnight, then." She nodded to each of them before entering her and Jathan's room. *Lord, please let this go well.*

TWENTY

*J*athan rose from the table, certain he'd heard the jostling of a buggy.

"What is it?" Sarah asked as she set her napkin next to her dinner plate.

"Someone's here. You and the girls may continue with supper." He walked through the living room and peered out the window. *What are Deacon Miller and Minister Zook doing here?*

He continued to watch as the deacon motioned toward Sarah's vehicle and exchanged a few words with Minister Zook. No doubt they'd heard of Sarah's return, although she'd yet to attend meeting with him. He knew this meeting was inevitable, but he'd hoped to put it off for as long as possible.

Jathan glanced back to the table and grimaced. The leaders certainly wouldn't approve of Sarah wearing worldly clothes. They'd already discussed the issue between themselves, and Sarah had agreed to wear her Amish clothing to meeting. But Jathan hadn't wanted to push the issue. He was just so thrilled to have Sarah back home, little else mattered to him. But now, what would he say to the leaders?

He stepped outside. Hopefully, this visit would be short and they'd be on their merry way. Not that Jathan didn't want to be hospitable. He just didn't want the leaders to offend Sarah. He'd been without her for so long, he couldn't risk losing her again.

"Jathan." The deacon nodded a greeting.

Jathan shook both men's hands.

"I see you have a car," the minister spoke in their native language.

"It's my wife's," Jathan explained.

"So, it is true. Jathan's Sarah has returned." The deacon stroked his beard.

"*Jah.*" Jathan lifted a nervous smile.

"May we speak with her?"

Jathan had hoped they wouldn't ask yet. He felt like saying no. "About what?"

Deacon Miller raised a brow. "What are her intentions? Is she going to stay? Will she join the church?"

Jathan frowned. "I don't know if she's ready to answer those questions yet."

"You know she is in the *Bann*. She left you, remember? You know a kneeling confession is required if she is to return."

"She was sick, in an accident. She would have returned to me but she lost her memory."

By his expression, Deacon Miller clearly believed nothing Jathan had just said.

"For ten years?" Minister Zook frowned. "And *you* believe this?"

"Of course, I believe it! Sarah's my wife." What nerve these men had, insinuating Sarah was a liar.

Deacon Miller sighed. "Calm down, Jathan. This does sound pretty far-fetched, if you think about it."

"My wife is not a liar," Jathan insisted.

"You're welcome to believe that."

"So, what are you saying? You want proof?" Jathan had always considered himself a calm man, but he felt none of it right now.

The two men looked at each other.

"If there *is* any." Minister Zook shrugged.

Jathan's hands clenched at his sides. He held his tongue.

"We'll return next week then. That should give you enough time to figure things out." Deacon Miller looked toward the house and shook his head.

Jathan turned to see Sarah and the girls standing at

the door. Hopefully, Sarah hadn't understood any of their exchange. In this moment, Jathan was thankful Sarah didn't remember her Pennsylvania Dutch.

Both of the men waved as they stepped back into the buggy and set it in motion.

Good riddance.

It had been days since the two Amish men had visited and Jathan still hadn't mentioned the reason they'd stopped by. He'd seemed very upset, so Sarah didn't want to aggravate him even more by inundating him with questions. Whatever it was, it seemed serious.

Jathan had been more quiet than usual and had kept to himself the past few days. Sarah wished he would talk to her. She didn't like the idea of him carrying his burdens alone. It wasn't healthy.

Sarah picked up her dusting rag and continued cleaning the bureau in their room. She lifted Jathan's Bible, intrigued by its uniqueness. It was written in German, she presumed, by the foreign words and Martin Luther's name inside. Something else within the pages caught her eye as she carefully thumbed through. It was a certificate of Holy Matrimony, the first solid proof she'd seen of their marriage vows, other than Jathan's word. Not that she doubted him for a moment. If only she could remember how she'd felt on that day. Had it been the best day of her life? Did she have doubts and fears about the future?

A turn of the pages revealed yet another treasure. She wondered if anyone other than Jathan had ever seen it. She stared at a photograph of her and Jathan, apparently as teenagers. Jathan was clean shaven and even more handsome than she'd imagined. No wonder she'd fallen for him. With his considerate personality and his good looks, how could she have resisted?

She stared at the photo a good five minutes before returning it to its place of honor in Jathan's Bible. How many times had he reminisced over this photo during the past ten years? Had he ever regretted marrying an *Englisch* girl? If they knew back then how their future would unfold, would they do it all over again? Now that was a question.

Sarah closed Jathan's Bible, lest she completely lose interest in cleaning the house. She placed the Bible back on the shelf, then glanced at it. Was that an envelope protruding from the Bible's back cover? Curiosity got the better of her and she picked up the Bible once again.

She pulled the envelope from inside the Bible's cover. Would Jathan mind her looking inside? She removed several folded lined papers from the envelope. Were they letters of some kind? Her eyes glued to the papers in her hands.

Dear Sarah, I wish I could tell you how much I want to get to know you. You are beautiful, and not just on the outside. Your smile and your words all say what I already know. It's no wonder that you are already taken. I know this is just a dream, but maybe someday, if it's Der Herr's will, we can be together. I will keep praying that He will make a way for us. Jathan Stolzfus

Dear Sarah, thank you for agreeing to let me court you, or at least for a date. I will do my best to care for you and treat you right. Don't worry about riding in my buggy. Jumper is a really good buggy horse and he can go slow if I make him. I can't wait to see you again. Saturday night can't come soon enough. Best, Jathan

Dear Sarah, every day that I'm with you, I fall in love with you even more. I love everything about you and I hope that someday you and I can get married. You own my heart. If something were to ever happen to you, I don't know what I'd do. I hope we can be together forever. I hope you feel the same way too. Yours alone, Jathan

Dear Sarah, I'm saddened that your folks don't approve of me. I don't know what I can do to make them like me. I will pray that we will find a way to be together. Maybe they will change their minds? All I know is that I love you and I don't want to be without you. I can't imagine ever loving anyone else as much as I love you. Yours alone, Jathan

Dear Sarah, I cannot tell you how happy I am that you said yes to marrying me. I promise you I'll be the best husband you could want. I'll give you anything you want. You already have my heart. I will never love another. Your Beloved, Jathan

Dear Sarah, Today is the second-best day of my life. Our little Sarah Joy was born! She's just as beautiful as her momma. Hopefully, Der Herr *will see fit to bless us with many* bopplin. *I know you will be a good momma. I love you more than words can say. Your Beloved, Jathan*

Dear Sarah, I don't know what I'd do without you. Losing Momma was one of the hardest things I've ever had to deal with. I know you loved and miss her too. Thank you for being there for me. My heart still aches greatly, but having you at my side makes life much more bearable. I feel sorry for Dat, *because I couldn't imagine how my life would be without you. You and the* kinner *mean so much to me. Your Beloved, Jathan*

Dear Sarah, I'm so ashamed of myself. What kind of Amish man falls off a roof? I'm glad that you will never see these letters because then you'll realized what a dummkopp *your husband is. I'll be up and around and working real soon, so don't you worry none. You'll see. Your Beloved, Jathan*

Dear Sarah, please forgive me! I've been such a dummkopp. *My heart is so full of aching and I know yours is too. I know we will never get our* boppli *back. I have failed you. I'm so sorry. I hope I won't lose you too. I need you. Please, forgive me. Your Beloved, Jathan*

Dear Sarah, I don't know what to write to you—not that you're here to read my words.

You've gone away and it's all my fault. From the day we first met, I was afraid this would happen—that you would leave me and go back to the Englisch. *Oh, Sarah, I don't know how I can go on without you by my side. Please come back to me and the* maed. *Please. They already miss you and you've only been gone two days yet. They ask me where Momma is and when she's coming home. Those are questions only you have the answers to. Not that it matters to you now, but I've stopped drinking. I know that is part of why you left. I know you must hate me but I'm asking for your forgiveness. If only I could go back and erase the last year and start it over again. I would do many things different. But I can't do that. There's nothing I can do to fix what's broken. And I'm afraid there's nothing I can do to bring you home, but I will try to find you. I will find you and beg for you to come home. I don't know how I'll go on without you, but I must for our girls' sake. I'm at a loss of what to do. I'd give anything to have you home again. Your Beloved, Jathan*

Dear Sarah, I don't know why I still write to you or why I still look for you every day. There is an ache in my heart that will never be filled. Oh, if only you'd come back home! If only you could forgive the past and we could start again. Our girls are getting bigger every day. Our Sarah Joy is almost finished with her schooling. I wish you could be here to teach her all the things she'll need to know to be a gut *Amish wife like her momma was. The* maed *still miss their momma although they talk about you less now. I hope they don't ever forget you. I know I never will. Even if you return to me when I'm old and grey, I will consider it the greatest blessing I will ever receive. Oh, how I do still love you! You will always be the only one for me. I hope your heart has healed, Sarah. I'm hoping beyond hope and praying with all that is in me that* Der Herr *will guide you back home to me. Your Beloved, Jathan*

Sarah folded the last letter and brushed the tears from her eyes and cheeks. What kind of life had Jathan and the girls lived without her? The sorrow of the realization that she abandoned them struck her hard. She'd left willingly. Would she have come back on her own, given different circumstances? Would she and Jathan still be married today or would she have divorced him? How different had she been back then?

Those were questions she'd never know the answers to.

Jathan had said in his letters that he prayed that God would lead her back home. It seems like that was exactly what happened. But why did God wait so long to answer his prayers? Why did He allow her to marry another man and cause Jathan pain for all those years? Was it because Jathan needed to learn a lesson? And what about Mark and the girls? What did they ever do to deserve being caught in the middle of this mess?

Sarah squeezed her eyes shut and tried with all her might to recall more memories. Nothing. No more memories had resurfaced since she remembered the birth of their baby boy, and even that memory was foggy. She wondered if there was a specific reason she recalled that event. Perhaps she'd have to talk to Jathan about it more. Not being able to remember was frustrating, especially now that she realized the volume of the memories she'd lost. Would talking to Jathan more help her remember the past?

"Momma?" Anna peeked her head through the door. "Someone's here to see you."

Sarah quickly hid the letters behind her back, hoping Anna hadn't seen them. "Okay, I'll be out in a minute."

"It's Aunt Ruth," Anna added, just before closing the door.

Sarah placed the letters back into Jathan's Bible and picked up her dusting rag. Her chores would have to wait until a more convenient time.

TWENTY-ONE

Ruth sipped on the hot apple cider Sarah had offered her just a few moments before. "I hope this is a good time for you." Ruth smiled.

"Oh, it's fine. I was dusting, but that can wait. Visiting is much more fun," Sarah said.

"I agree." Ruth laughed. "How are you adjusting to Amish life again?"

Sarah shrugged. "I don't know if it's fully dawned on me yet. It's a lot of work, doing everything by hand and without electricity."

"I can imagine it would be difficult after living an *Englisch* lifestyle for so long."

"Yeah. I used to just buy pie crust already made from the store and dump the can of apples in. Now I have to buy all the ingredients, roll out the dough, cut the apples and cook them, mix in all the spices, and then put it into the oven. I admit, I'm not used to it.

My first couple of pies turned out pretty crude looking."

"But I bet they tasted good."

"You know, they did, actually."

"You'll get the hang of it. A *boppli* don't start out walkin' the day she's born."

"I guess you have a point."

"I'll tell you a secret." Ruth lifted a finger to her lips. "I don't always make my own pie crust." She winked.

Sarah smiled and winked back. "I won't tell if you won't."

Ruth's smile vanished and her gaze met Sarah's. "Have the leaders come by to talk to you yet?"

"Jathan spoke with a couple of Amish men that stopped by the other day, but he didn't say who they were. They both had beards, one grey and one brown."

Ruth nodded. "Must've been Deacon Miller and Minister Zook. Were you wearing these clothes?"

Sarah looked down at her jeans. "Yeah. Well, not these exact clothes but something similar. Why do you ask?"

"Did they see you?"

"I was standing at the door when they left." Sarah shrugged. "I guess they may have."

Ruth shook her head. "If they did see you in *Englisch* clothes, I'm certain sure Jathan got a talking to. Especially if your car was out there yet."

Sarah frowned. "Jathan will be punished because of my clothes? And my car? I don't understand."

"Jathan has not spoken with you about these things?"

"We did talk about me wearing my Amish dress to church on Sunday."

Ruth sighed. "I will have to talk to my brother. He knows better."

"I don't understand. Am I doing something wrong?"

"Sarah, you are still under the *Bann* as far as I know."

"The bon? I'm not sure I know what that means." Hadn't Jathan mentioned something about that when she was talking about them sharing their faith with the leaders?

"You are shunned. *Ach*, Jathan. He should have told you these things."

"*I* am shunned? Explain to me exactly what that is because I don't think I'm getting what you say." Perhaps Ruth had a more in-depth explanation than Jathan had given her.

"When you left, the leaders of the church voted to

put you in the *Bann*. That means that you may not have close fellowship with anyone in our community. You are to sit at a different table for meals. No one is allowed to accept anything from your hand. No one is allowed to ride in your car. Jathan may not sleep in the same bed as you. All your gifts must be refused."

She and Jathan weren't allowed to sleep together? Or eat together? Apparently, Jathan had disobeyed the leaders in allowing these things. Perhaps he didn't agree with them. "What is the reasoning behind all this? It doesn't make sense."

"Sarah, when you left, you forsook your vows to Jathan and to the church. It is better not to make a vow at all, then to make a vow and break it."

"That's from the Bible."

"*Jah*. And so is the *Bann*. We are to have no fellowship with an unbeliever or disobedient one."

"So, is that what they think? That I'm disobedient? I don't even know what all the rules are. How can I keep rules I don't even know about?"

"You knew about them before you left. And you *did* leave willingly."

Sarah swallowed the lump in her throat. "Ruth, did Jathan tell you about my accident? That I lost my memory?"

"*Jah*."

"Do the leaders know?"

"I imagine that Jathan would have told them."

Sarah felt moisture gathering in her eyes. "Well, my coming back is like entering into another world. This is all new to me. I need some time to adjust. They can't expect me to just become a perfect Amish woman overnight."

Ruth sighed. "I agree with you, Sarah. But at some point, the leaders will expect you to make a kneeling confession, you know."

Sarah shook her head. "No, I don't know. What does a kneeling confession involve?"

"*Ach.* I probably shouldn't even be the one telling you all this. That Jathan." She scolded her brother as though he were present.

"Please, Ruth. I want to know."

"You will have to go before the congregation and confess your transgressions."

Sarah's eyes almost popped out. "Confess my transgressions? I thought that was just a Catholic thing."

"If you want to be restored back into the fellowship, that is what is required."

"You're serious." Sarah frowned.

"I would not lie to you about these things."

"No, I know you wouldn't. I'm just...what would

I confess? I can't even begin to imagine what they would want me to say."

"Sarah, that would be between you and *Der Herr*. The leaders just want a true confession. They want to know whether you will leave again or no. And rest assured, they will be watching you."

"They're watching me? That sounds ominous. It reminds me of Big Brother."

"Big Brother?"

"You know, the government."

"They are not part of the government," Ruth insisted.

"Oh, no. I didn't mean... Never mind, it was kind of a joke."

"Well, your confession will be no joke. It is very serious."

"But what if what I say isn't good enough for them? Then what?"

"*Ach*, Sarah. You worry too much about these things. Give it to *Gott* and ask Him to show you what to say." Ruth sipped her cider, a corner of her mouth lifting slightly. "You and Jathan seem to be getting along *gut*. You look happy."

Sarah smiled, relieved to have a change in subject. "*Jah*. We are."

"Do you love him, Sarah?"

Sarah hadn't really considered the reply to Ruth's seemingly simple question until now. She pondered everything that had taken place since discovering she was Jathan's wife. She was definitely physically attracted to him. It was clear that Jathan possessed undying devotion for her—that was evident in everything he did. But did she have the same dedication to him?

"Sarah?"

She met Ruth's gaze and offered the most honest answer she could. "I believe I do."

A satisfied smile replaced Ruth's hesitant expression from a moment before. "I'm glad to hear it. So, you will stay with Jathan now?"

Sarah smiled and nodded. "I have no plans to leave. Mark and I have gotten an annulment, and he moved up to Maine. I am Jathan's wife. This is my home now."

"*Gut, gut.* That is what the leaders will want to hear."

"Do you think they'll have anything against Mark's and my girls coming to stay here?"

Ruth's mouth fell open. "You have other *kinner*?"

"Jathan didn't tell you?"

"*Nee.* I didn't know," she huffed.

"Yes. Mark and I have two daughters. They are

with him right now, but they will live with us half the year."

"I do not know what the leaders will say. I'm for sure and certain they've never had to deal with something like this."

"You don't think they would forbid it, do you?"

Ruth shrugged. "I don't know, Sarah."

Sarah swallowed the lump in her throat, determined not to let fear overpower her mind. But, what if the leaders refused to let her daughters come and stay? She couldn't just forsake Brooke and Claire. What would she do?

God, please take this situation into Your hands. You know I can't abandon my daughters. Please help me to find favor with the leaders.

TWENTY-TWO

athan maneuvered the horse and buggy to the hitching post near the barn and waved to beautiful Sarah, who hung laundry on the line. Normally, the women in their community hung laundry on Mondays. He smiled. It would take some time for Sarah to adjust to the Amish lifestyle again. And that was fine with him.

He had yet to talk to Sarah about the minister and deacon's visit, because he was worried about placing too much stress on her shoulders. But now, he needed to say something, lest the leaders return to talk to her.

He quickly unloaded the supplies he'd purchased, and released the driving horse into a barn stall. Once he rinsed his hands under the outside pump, he moved toward his wife. This was certainly his favorite time of day. Just coming home and knowing that she'd be there to greet him with a kiss and a smile was like a little piece of Heaven.

Jathan walked up behind Sarah quietly and gently slipped his arms around her waist. Sarah turned in his arms and rewarded him with the kiss he'd been dreaming about all day.

"Thank you." He smiled. "Come, let's go for a walk."

"But I'm not finished with the laundry."

"It can wait. It won't walk away." He chuckled.

"Okay, if you insist."

"We'll go down yonder in a bit, but I should show you something first." Jathan led the way to an area just beyond the back yard, where a small white picket fence formed a rectangle. He lifted the latch on the gate and gestured for Sarah to enter.

Sarah's eyes met his. "Our baby's grave?" Her eyes immediately filled with tears.

"*Jah.*" He swallowed, remembering the anguish they'd both felt the day the baby was laid to rest. He'd relived the words Sarah had spoken to him many times—words he wished he could forget.

"Did we give him a name?" She continued staring at the tiny grave.

Yes, you named him. "It's on the other side."

She moved to see the inscription, squatting next to the tiny grave marker. "Jathan," Sarah looked up at him. "We named him after you?"

"*You* did." He couldn't help the edge in his tone.

Sarah frowned. "Did you not approve of his name?"

"I'd rather not talk about it."

"Jathan, it's obviously something that's bothered you for some time, so I think we should."

"*Nee.*"

"Jathan, what happened? Please, I want to know. Since I can't remember, you have to help me fill in the details."

Jathan looked toward the house. Maybe this wasn't the best idea. "You'd be better off not knowing."

"I want to know."

He sighed. "Fine, if you insist. I wanted to name him Sebastian, after my father," he spat out. "You said, 'No, your father is still alive. We'll name him Jathan, because he is dead just like his father is to me.'"

"I said that to you?" Sarah covered her mouth.

Jathan crossed his arms and stared out at the field. He stayed silent, lest he lose his composure.

"Jathan, I really said that to you?" Her eyes clouded once again. "I'm *so* sorry. And you've lived with those words all these years. How could I do that to you?" She shook her head. "I don't know what to say. I'm sure I couldn't have meant it."

"You did mean it. And you proved it when you left. But that's okay. I deserved it."

"No, it's not okay. Please forgive me, Jathan. I must've been talking out of grief." She frowned. "Have you ever heard of postpartum depression?"

"*Nee.*"

"It's quite common. Sometimes, after a woman has a baby, she gets depressed. It is usually due to an imbalance in hormones. And it happens to many women—even when there is no baby lost. I'm sure I didn't mean those words. We'd just lost a baby. I wasn't in my right mind."

Could it be possible that Sarah was telling the truth? That she really hadn't meant those words?

"I'm not excusing myself. I know I never should have said those words in the first place." She touched his shoulder. "Jathan, I need your forgiveness. Please."

"But you were right. It was my fault. The *boppli* would still be alive if it wasn't for me."

"You need to let go of your guilt, Jathan. Maybe what you did was wrong. And what I said was wrong. But that's all in our past. There's nothing we can do to change that. We can't go back and do it over again. Besides, if God wanted our baby to live, He would have seen fit to keep him alive. Instead, for whatever reason, God chose to take him to Heaven." Sarah stood up and came to him. She cradled his face in her hands. "Baby, you've got to let this go. Give it to God."

How he hated feeling vulnerable in front of Sarah. "I'll try." He swallowed back the lump in his throat.

"Does that mean you'll forgive me?"

He nodded and kissed her cheek. "How can I not?"

"Thank you, Jathan." She met his lips but it ended too quickly. "Now, you wanted to show me something else?"

"*Jah*. Come." He took her by the hand and led her down the path toward the stream that flowed through their property. A few years ago, Jathan had added a park bench so they'd have a place to rest. "Sit."

Sarah did as suggested. "This is beautiful."

He removed his hat and ran his fingers through his hair. "We need to talk about some other things too."

Sarah nodded in agreement. Was there something she wanted to say as well?

He took a seat next to her. "Do you remember when the two Amish men stopped by a few days ago?"

"Yes."

"Well, that was Deacon Miller and Minister Zook." Jathan sighed.

"What did they want?"

"They asked about you. They wanted to know

what your intentions are."

Sarah frowned. "My *intentions*?"

"*Jah*. They seem worried because of your car and your clothes. I...Sarah, I'd like to give you more time to adjust but I'm afraid the leaders are not willing to wait so long."

"I haven't even been here two weeks."

"I know." He swallowed. "We need to discuss some things."

Sarah nodded in silence, but he couldn't read her expression.

He might as well just spell it out. There was no use postponing the inevitable. "We will need to sell your car soon. And I think it would be best if you start wearing your Amish clothes."

"Okay."

Okay? That wasn't the reaction he'd expected. "You...you are fine with this?"

"Jathan, this is my home now. You and the girls are my family. I plan to do my part."

Another reason why he loved her. "Sarah, I can't begin to tell you how much..." He swallowed. "Thank you."

But there was yet another topic to be discussed— one he'd been dreading even more.

Sarah smiled. "Ruth stopped by today."

"She did?"

Sarah nodded.

"Did you have a nice visit?"

"Yes. I like your sister. She brought up some things, though."

"What things?"

"The *Bann*."

He nodded in silence.

"Jathan, why haven't you told me that I've been excommunicated?"

He shrugged. "I wanted to wait until the time was right."

"And until then we just continue breaking the rules? Jathan, we're not allowed to eat together. Or sleep together."

He shook his head. "I refuse to shun my own wife. I won't do it."

"But won't you get in trouble with the leaders?"

"I'd rather be in the *Bann* with you, than free from it without you. *Der Herr* says what *Gott* has joined together, let no man put asunder. I believe that includes our leaders. They cannot separate us. I love you, Sarah."

"I love you too, Jathan."

The words melted his heart. "I'm so blessed to have you as my wife. You are more than I ever hoped for and so much more than I deserve."

"I feel the same way about you."

"You do?"

"Jathan, you have the purest heart I've ever known."

"*Ach*, don't say that."

"It's true. The way you love and care for me and the girls is beyond compare. It's easy to love you."

"Sarah, I never dreamed..." Jathan hastily wiped his eye. "*Der Herr* has been so *gut* to me." He reached for his wife and drew her close. If only he'd known during the ten years of her absence that their relationship could be restored, and that he'd be able to hold her in his arms and kiss her lips like this again, it would have made the pain so much more bearable. He'd felt like such a failure then, and he didn't think his world would ever be right again. But that time was behind them now, and here they were. Just when he'd nearly lost all hope.

This was truly the work of the Lord.

TWENTY-THREE

Today was the day. It would be the first day she attended an Amish church service since she'd been back. It had taken her over an hour to get dressed and pin her hair up. It was a good thing she didn't have to apply her makeup as well. After wearing it for so many years, she felt almost naked without it.

Sarah looked into the mirror on the bureau, the light from the window reflecting off her red tinted hair. Would the leaders require her to dye it back to its natural color? It was something she and Jathan had already discussed. Jathan said he didn't mind and that she looked beautiful either way. She smiled at the thought. But she was pretty certain that he probably preferred her natural color, whether he admitted it or not.

She placed the pretty heart-shaped prayer *kapp*

over her bun and frowned. Oh, no. It was too small. Or maybe she'd done her bun wrong. She quickly took her hair down and attempted to figure out exactly where it needed to be for the *kapp* to fit properly. After a few frustrating tries, she finally got it right. She sighed and quickly fastened the *kapp* with a few straight pins, taking special care not to stick them into her head like she'd done with the metal hair pins a few moments ago.

So this was what she'd looked like the first eight years of her and Jathan's marriage, huh? Minus the dyed hair, of course. She briefly wondered how long it took her to get ready back then. Surely not—she glanced at the clock on the wall—an hour and a half.

Well, Jathan said that they only had meeting once every other week, fortunately. But the girls wore their *kapps,* or some kind of head covering at least, every day. Maybe she'd just wear a handkerchief on non-church days like the girls sometimes did.

Sarah smoothed her dress and apron, and glanced into the mirror one more time before leaving the room and presenting herself to her family. Boy, did she look different. Plain Sarah. She wondered if she'd even recognize herself if she were someone else walking on the street. *Not likely.*

Sarah walked into the kitchen, where Jathan and

the girls sat around the table. "Well, what do you think?" She spun around once and laughed.

Jathan seemed to be unable to take his eyes off her. "My beautiful Sarah, my *fraa*." Just seeing the expression on Jathan's face made it all worth it. His glistening eyes didn't escape her notice, either.

"*Ach*, Momma, you look *schee!*" Sarah Joy exclaimed. The other girls' smiles agreed.

Jathan reached for her hand and pulled her close. "Close your eyes, girls, so I can kiss your momma."

"Eww!"

Sarah laughed as Julie, the youngest, quickly covered her eyes.

৵৵৵

Sarah was certain she must've been the talk of the community since she showed up on the scene. Every single person at their Amish church meeting seemed to want to take a gander at Jathan's wayward *fraa*. Not that she could blame them. If it were someone else's situation, she would probably be curious too. But even so, being the center of attention wasn't the most comfortable thing in the world.

She and Jathan hadn't discussed the church service much, so she was unsure of what to expect. She knew it would be quite different from the *Englisch* church services she'd attended the last five years of her life, but she never realized *how* different it would be. Thankfully, upon her arrival, Ruth clued her in on where to sit and what to do. Although she'd expected to sit next to Jathan, she wasn't surprised when Ruth instructed her to sit on the opposite side of the room with all of the other women.

The acapella singing threw her off, especially since each word of the song was several seconds in length. It almost seemed like a chant of sorts to her ears. The songbook, which Ruth had called the *Ausbund*, had no musical notation so she had no idea how the songs were to be sung. Not to mention, they were all written in German.

Fortunately, some of the preaching was in English. After about two hours of sitting on the hard wooden bench, Sarah felt like getting up and walking around. Where did Ruth say the restroom was located? Would it be improper or rude for her to get up and find it? Her eyes began surveying the different rooms in the Bylers' home. Just as she determined to find a restroom, the congregation turned and kneeled in front of the benches they'd been sitting on. She sighed and decided to wait a little bit longer. Perhaps the service was almost done.

Sarah eyed the many women bustling to prepare the food for the common meal, her sister-in-law, being one of them. The men worked to move the benches and fix the tables for the meal.

"Ruth, what can I do to help?" Sarah smiled.

"*Ach*, Sarah, you are not allowed to. You may not serve. You are in the *Bann*, remember?"

Sarah's jaw dropped and she frowned. *I'm not even allowed to help serve? Wow, this shunning thing is harsh.*

Jathan had informed Sarah earlier during their buggy ride to meeting that they would not sit together during the common meal. Just as they had in the church service, the men and women sat separately. As a matter of fact, she was expected to sit separate from the other women as well. They were not allowed to fellowship with her.

Sarah wondered what she should do while everyone else busied themselves with work. Perhaps a walk would do her good. No telling how long the meal and fellowshipping would last. She looked over at Jathan, who sat eating and talking with a group of other Amish men. His laughter filled the air and lifted a smile from Sarah's lips. Their girls were helping serve the meal, except for Sarah Joy, who spoke with a couple of friends in the side yard.

Sarah set off on foot down the Bylers' driveway, since there appeared to be nothing for her to do. At least she could get a little exercise and enjoy the countryside a bit. The weather was nippy but she'd brought along a warm coat. The walk was a nice break from all the bustling in the kitchen, and the quiet calmed her soul. She breathed in the fresh wintry air but it brought a chill. She rubbed her hands together and pulled her parka a little tighter.

Jathan surveyed the room as he took his paper towel to the trash can. The girls had already eaten and were now gathered around the tables chatting with their friends. Where was Sarah? Jathan searched the house but saw no sign of her. He hasted outside and found various groups of men and women, but Sarah was nowhere to be seen.

He found his sister. "Ruth, have you seen Sarah?"

She shook her head. "Not since before the meal a couple of hours ago."

A couple of hours ago? Jathan chided himself for not being more attentive to his wife. *Where could she be?* He continued searching the Bylers' property and asked everyone he came across. No one had seen her.

Jathan had never considered himself a worrier, but

since the time Sarah disappeared ten years ago, he'd had a little practice in that department. A million different scenarios ran through his head. What if Sarah left again? What if being around the Amish community was too much for her and she decided she'd rather stay *Englisch*? She couldn't have walked home, could she? It was too far and the weather was too cold. *God, where could she be?*

After searching the property one more time with no results, Jathan decided to go looking for her. He found Ruth again and asked her to keep an eye on the girls until he returned with Sarah. He would find her. He had to.

TWENTY-FOUR

Sarah pulled her gloves out of her pocket and slipped them on. The temperature felt like it had dropped ten degrees since she'd left the Bylers'. How long had she been gone, anyway? Maybe she should begin heading back.

Sarah turned around and began walking the way she'd come. A snowflake hit her nose. Then another. And another. She picked up her pace, lest she get caught in a blizzard. It wasn't likely, since this was the first snow she'd seen this year, but just in case.

She came to the end of the country road and looked both ways. Which direction had she come from? She looked at the ground for her footprints, but there was no trace of them. They'd all been covered by the snow. *This is great!*

Maybe she should have told Jathan she was going for a walk. Of course, it was too late now. But if he'd known which way she'd gone, at least he would know which direction to search for her.

As the snowflakes became denser and fell harder, Sarah decided she'd better find shelter somewhere. She squinted to attempt to see through the flurry of white. *Which direction am I going?* There had been a fence down the road a little ways, hadn't there? Perhaps she could find it and feel her way toward civilization. All she knew is that she better find shelter quickly before she turned into a human snowman.

Jathan cringed the moment he stepped outside. It was no wonder there were so many people inside the Bylers' home. He had no idea it had begun snowing. *Ach, Sarah.*

He hated to admit to anyone that Sarah was missing because he didn't want to invite gossip. But with Sarah's life possibly at stake, he wasn't going to take any chances.

"John, may I speak to you for a minute?" Jathan called his brother-in-law to the door. Thankfully, he and his family hadn't left yet.

"Sure. You need something?" His brother-in-law, just a couple of years younger than Jathan, scratched his sandy-colored beard.

"It's my *fraa*, Sarah. I think she must've gone for a walk or headed home. I can't find her anywhere." Could John detect the concern in his voice?

"I see." He glanced at his wife, who spoke with another Amish woman in their community. "Let me talk to Ruthie."

Jathan stood by the door as patiently as he possibly could. He hurried to his oldest daughter. "Sarah Joy, I'm gonna go with Uncle John and look for your *mamm*. You keep an eye on the others for me, okay?"

Sarah Joy frowned. "Where's Momma?"

"I don't know. I think she just went for a walk. It shouldn't take me long to find her." Was he trying to convince his daughter or himself? He hoped Sarah Joy wasn't as worried as he was. The girls had already experienced more turmoil in the last ten years than anyone should in a lifetime. They didn't need any more. "I'll be back as soon as I can."

Sarah Joy looked to the window, where the snow was falling even harder now. "Hurry, *Daed!*"

Jathan rushed to the door and John met him at the same time. "I'm not going to hitch up the buggy. I'll ride bareback."

His brother-in-law brought his hat lower. "Are you sure, Jathan?"

"*Jah*. You go ahead and hitch up if you want to.

I'm heading this way." Jathan pointed in the direction of his home, the most logical direction Sarah would have gone if she was heading back to the house.

"I'll go the other direction."

Before John could hitch up his buggy, Jathan was already headed down the road. He pulled his coat tighter, glad for his hat and the scarf Sarah had crocheted for him many years ago. It was something he'd always cherished, and when Sarah disappeared ten years ago, he'd put it away for safe keeping. This was the first time he'd taken it out and worn it since then.

"Sarah!" Jathan called, as he rode slowly along the snow-covered country lane. There was no telling where she could be. He had to find her. There was no way he was going to lose her again.

Jathan wasn't certain how long he'd been out riding, but it had surely been over an hour. Still, there was no sign of Sarah. Maybe she was already at the house or back at the Bylers'. Or perhaps John had found her.

It was times like this he wished he and others in their community could own a cell phone. *Cell phone!* Sarah still had a phone. Did she have it with her? He rode a little further and stopped at the nearest phone shanty he could find. With nearly numb fingers, he dialed her number. He'd memorized it as soon as she'd given it to him. That was the day she'd first shown up at the house with Mark. Little did he know, his precious wife would return to him and their relationship would be restored. At the time, it had seemed impossible.

Her phone rang twice and then went to her voicemail. "Sarah, this is Jathan. I'm looking for you right now, so wherever you're at just stay there. I'll find you." He spoke with much more confidence than he felt.

Jathan decided the best thing to do was to go check the house. If she'd gone anywhere, it would've been there. As he pulled into the yard, everything looked as it had before, the snow notwithstanding. His first notion was to check the barn. He rolled open the sliding door. A sigh of relief escaped his lips. Never in his life had he been happier to see a car.

He closed the barn door and rushed to the house. "Sarah, are you in here, *schatzi*?" he called. "Sarah?" He listened for a few minutes but heard nothing of significance.

He quickly shed his coat and slipped into a warmer, dry one. He also found a pair of gloves. If Sarah was still out in this awful weather, she had to be freezing.

Jennifer Spredemann

With that in mind, he snatched a few items of clothing from her drawers, including a warm pair of socks.

God, please let John have found her already.

Twenty minutes later, Jathan arrived back at the Bylers' farm. John's buggy had been returned to the barn, but the buggy was still hitched to the horse. Jathan hurried inside, hoping Sarah would be present and safe and sound with the others.

"John, did you find Sarah?" Jathan called from the kitchen door while stomping the snow off his boots.

"*Nee.* No sign of her. I was hoping you'd found her."

Jathan shook his head. Why was it that, in times of trouble, trusting God seemed so difficult for him? Maybe because he felt unworthy of *Der Herr's* help?

"You didn't find Momma?" Tears struck Sarah Joy's eyes as she maneuvered her wheelchair into the kitchen. "You have to find her, *Daed.*"

"We will," John assured.

Jathan nodded to his brother-in-law. "John, will you give the girls a ride home for me? I don't plan to return home until I find Sarah." This felt eerily similar to the days he'd gone searching for her while she was missing.

"Where do you suppose she could be?" Ruth frowned.

"You said you last saw her before the meal, right?" Jathan asked.

John frowned. "That was several hours ago. She could be anywhere by now."

"You don't think she left you again, do you?" Minister Zook said.

"*Nee*," Jathan spat out. If he didn't hold to his Amish values so strongly, he could have sent the heartless minister home with more than just leftovers from the common meal. Jathan clenched his hands.

"Momma said she's staying with us now," Becky added. "Daddy, you have to find her."

"She's probably scared out in the snow all by herself." Julie's eyes grew wide.

Jathan smiled at the girls and reassured them. "She's not by herself. *Der Herr* is with her. He will lead me to your momma." *God, please let it be so.*

The minister raised an eyebrow. "Shall we call the men of the community to help you look for your *fraa*...again?"

"Not yet. I intend to find her myself." Jathan turned to the girls. "You go with Uncle John and make sure to put some wood on the fire."

"We will, *Daed*," Anna said. "And we'll make some coffee for when you bring Momma home."

"*Denki*. You do that." Jathan smiled. "I'll be home

with your momma just as soon as I can."

Ruth handed her brother an insulated beverage container along with a plastic bag. "Here, take some hot tea and snacks with you. She probably hasn't eaten anything."

"*Denki*, Ruth. You're the best." Jathan nodded.

"I know." Jathan heard his sister's teasing tone as he opened the back door, and he shook his head. Sometimes he missed the days when he and his siblings were young and still at home. Those were precious memories he'd always carry with him.

He moved to the barn. It would probably be best to hitch up the buggy this time. He quickly slipped the traces into their leather holders and tightened the necessary straps on the harness, something he'd done since he was about five years old. In fact, he could probably do it in his sleep.

In no time, Jathan was back on the road again. He'd stop at every house this time and ask if the residents had seen Sarah. It was possible that someone may have spotted her out walking.

Sarah yawned and opened her eyes, a ray of light streamed through one of the old woodshed's rickety panels. She shivered at the nippy air, thankful she wasn't still out in the icy squall. But the wind had ceased whistling through the walls. Had the snow stopped falling?

She lifted her head from the corner beam it rested on and searched for the socks she'd removed from her wet feet. Hopefully they were dry by now. She reached for her shoes next to her, a pair of plain black tennis shoes, and felt to see if they were dry yet. She certainly hadn't expected them to be, not with the freezing temperatures. *Still wet.* Sarah frowned.

She rubbed her feet then placed the damp socks over them. They were cold, but it was better than going barefoot. Sarah stood and stretched. Maybe it would help get her circulation going if she did a few jumping jacks.

Who knew what time it was? Jathan was probably worried sick about her. She had to find her way back home—or at least to an Amish farm where they knew who she was. Or who Jathan was. But she was in the *Bann*. Would they even be allowed to give her a ride back home, or help her at all? Ruth had said that shunned members weren't allowed inside the house, in some cases. Would they leave her out in the cold? Being in the *Bann* was inconvenient, to say the least.

Relief flooded her when she stepped outside. Old Man Winter still nipped at her cheeks, but the snow had stopped and the wind had died down considerably. At least she could see where she was going. But now that everything was hidden under a blanket of white, nothing looked familiar. Nevertheless, the sheer beauty of the scenery nearly brought her to her knees in worship of her Saviour.

A swirl of smoke rising into the sky up ahead told her civilization was near. How far was the closest house? As Sarah walked along the road, she grimaced with each step as snow fell into her shoes once again. What she would give for a pair of warm, dry snow boots right now. She'd managed to avoid frostbite in the woodshed by removing her wet socks and shoes and warming her feet next to her bare skin under her coat. She ignored the pain from the cold and forced herself to keep going. Staring at the smoke up ahead and dreaming about sitting in front of a warm fire compelled her onward.

She turned slightly at the rattling sound behind her. *A buggy! God, please let it be Jathan,* she prayed in silence. Oh, to see Jathan again!

Jathan's heart turned a somersault when he spotted the Amish woman walking just up ahead. It had to be Sarah. He called to Driver, who was no doubt as tired as he was, and urged her forward with haste. If only she had wings.

"Sarah!" he hollered out the side buggy flap.

The woman stopped and turned around. *It's her!*

Another three hundred feet and he would catch up to her. He yanked on the reins and came to an abrupt stop. He hastened out of the buggy. His heart pounded louder with each step that drew closer to her.

Oh, to see her walk toward him!

Sarah's fierce embrace told him she was just as happy to see him. Neither one of them spoke for the first thirty seconds or so as they clung to each other.

"Sarah! Are you all right?" He kissed her lips and examined her clothing.

"My feet. They're turning numb."

"Come." He whisked her off her feet and carried her to the buggy. "Let's get you home."

"Thank you, Jathan." Tears welled in her eyes. "I'm sorry for not telling you that I was going for a walk. You were busy talking and—"

"*Nee*. It doesn't matter. All that matters is you're safe now." He rubbed her gloved hand. "It is my fault for not paying more attention to you. We shouldn't have stayed after church. I should have brought you home. I didn't consider, with you being in the *Bann*..." *Dummkopp*, he chided himself. "I don't ever want to lose you again."